A Brief History of Portable Literature

Enrique Vila-Matas

A Brief History
of Portable Literature

Translated from the Spanish
by Anne McLean & Thomas Bunstead

A NEW DIRECTIONS BOOK

This edition is published by arrangement with Enrique Vila-Matas c/o MB Agencia Literaria S.L.

Manufactured in the United States of America
New Directions Books are printed on acid-free paper
First published in 2015 as New Directions Paperbook 1308

Library of Congress Cataloging-in-Publication Data
Vila-Matas, Enrique, 1948–
[Historia abreviada de la literatura portátil. English]
A brief history of portable literature / Enrique Vila-Matas ; translated from the Spanish by Anne McLean and Thomas Bunstead. — First American paperback edition.
pages cm
"A New Directions book."
ISBN 978-0-8112-2337-9 (acid-free paper)
1. Literature, Modern—20th century—History and criticism. 2. Intellectual life—20th century. I. McLean, Anne, 1962– translator. II. Bunstead, Thomas, translator. III. Title.
PN778.V4813 2015
741.5'973—dc23   2014046884

10 9 8 7 6 5 4 3 2

New Directions Books are published for James Laughlin
by New Directions Publishing Corporation
80 Eighth Avenue, New York 10011

"The infinite, my dear friend, is no big deal—it's a matter of writing—the universe exists only on paper."

—Paul Valéry, *Monsieur Teste*

PROLOGUE

Toward the end of the winter of 1924, on the enormous, towering rock where the concept of eternal recurrence first came to Nietzsche, the Russian writer Andrei Bely suffered a nervous breakdown as he experienced the irremediably ascending lavas of the superconscious. On the same day, at the same time, a short distance away, the musician Edgar Varèse fell from his horse when, parodying Apollinaire, he pretended to set off for war.

For me these two scenes seem to be the pillars on which the history of portable literature is built: a history European in its origins and as light as the "desk-case" Paul Morand carried with him on luxury trains as he traveled the whole of an illuminated, nocturnal Europe. This moveable desk was the inspiration for Marcel Duchamp's *Boîte-en-valise*, indisputably the most brilliant bid to exalt portability in art. Duchamp's box-in-a-suitcase—which contained miniature reproductions of each his works—soon became an "anagram" for portable literature and the symbol by which the first Shandies* would come to be recognized.

Months later and with a minor alteration to the *boîte-en-valise* (a hairclip now serving as its clasp), this "anagram" would be

---

* Shandy, in the dialect of certain ridings of Yorkshire (where Laurence Sterne, the author of *Tristram Shandy*, lived for much of his life), can mean joyful as well as voluble or zany.

rearranged by Jacques Rigaut, who tried to represent, as he put it, the apotheosis of "featherweights" in the history of literature. His drawing was widely praised—perhaps for its markedly unorthodox character—and it prompted an extraordinary avalanche of new and daring corruptions of the Duchampian anagram, very clear evidence of the unremittingly transgressive impulse characterizing the first writers incorporated into the Shandy secret society.

Around the same time—and because of a widespread fear among those first Shandies that the box-in-a-suitcase might fall into the hands of any old charlatan—Walter Benjamin came up with a remarkably successful design for the joyous book-weighing machine that bears his name and allows us to judge, to this day, with unerring precision, which literary works are insupportable, and therefore—though they may try to disguise the fact—untransportable.

It's no coincidence that much of the originality of what was written by the inventor of the Benjamin machine can be attributed to his microscopic attention to detail (along with his unflagging command of philosophical theories). "It was the small things that he was most drawn to," his close friend Gershom Scholem wrote. Walter Benjamin had a fondness for old toys, postage stamps, photographic postcards, and those imitations of real winter landscapes contained within a glass globe where it snows when shaken.

Walter Benjamin's own handwriting was almost microscopic. His never-achieved ambition was to fit a hundred lines onto a single sheet of paper. Scholem says that the first time he visited Benjamin in Paris, his friend dragged him along to the Musée de Cluny to show him, in an exhibition of ritual Jewish objects, two grains of wheat upon which some kindred spirit had written out the entirety of the *Shema Yisrael*.

Walter Benjamin and Marcel Duchamp were kindred spirits. Both were vagrants, always on the move, exiled from the world of art, and, at the same time, collectors weighed down by many things—that is, by passions. Both knew that to miniaturize is to make portable, and for a vagrant and an exile, that is the best way of owning things.

But to miniaturize is also to conceal. Duchamp, for example, always felt drawn to extremely small things that cried out to be deciphered: insignia, manuscripts, symbols. For him, to miniaturize also meant to make "useless": "What is reduced finds itself in a sense liberated from meaning. Its smallness is, at one and the same time, a totality and a fragment. The love of small things is a childish emotion."

As childish as the perspective of Kafka who, as is well known, engaged in a struggle to the death to enter into paternal society, but would only have done so on the condition he could carry on being the irresponsible child he was.

The portable writers always behaved like irresponsible children. From the outset, they established staying single as an essential requirement for entering into the Shandy secret society or, at least, acting as though one were. That is, functioning in the manner of a "bachelor machine" in the sense Marcel Duchamp intended soon after learning—through Edgar Varèse no less—of Andrei Bely's nervous breakdown: "At that moment, I don't know why, I ceased listening to Varèse and began to think one shouldn't weigh life down excessively, with too many tasks, with what we call a wife, children, a house in the country, a car, etc. Happily, I came to understand this very early on. For a long time, I have lived as a bachelor much more easily than if I'd had to tackle all of life's normal difficulties. When it comes down to it, this is key."

That Duchamp should come to understand all of this just as Varèse was telling him of Bely's nervous breakdown on the enormous, towering rock of eternal recurrence is still strange. One inevitably wonders what link there might be between Bely's frayed nerves and the Duchampian resolve to remain single at all costs, daydreaming like all irresponsible children. It's hard—practically impossible—to know. Most likely there isn't any link at all, and the image of a celibate person (impossible, gratuitous, outrageous) simply occurred to Duchamp all of a sudden, unaccompanied by any explicable memory or conscious association. That's to say, a portable artist, or what amounts to the same thing, someone easy to carry around, wherever one goes.

Whatever happened, the one clear thing is that Varèse's fall, Bely's breakdown, and the unexpected emergence of a celibate, gratuitous, outrageous artist in Duchamp's field of vision were the pillars on which the Shandy secret society was based.

Two other essential requirements for being a member of this society (apart from the demand for high-grade madness) were established: along with the fact one's work mustn't weigh very much and should easily fit into a suitcase, the other essential condition was that of functioning in the manner of a "bachelor machine."

Though not essential, certain other typically Shandy-esque characteristics were also advisable: an innovative bent, an extreme sexuality, a disinterest in grand statements, a tireless nomadism, a fraught coexistence with doppelgängers, a sympathy for negritude, and the cultivation of the art of insolence.

In insolence, there is a swiftness of action, a proud spontaneity that smashes the old mechanisms, triumphing speedily over a powerful but sluggish enemy. From the outset, the Shandies decided that what they really wanted was for the portable conspiracy to become the stunning celebration of what appears and disappears with the arrogant velocity of the lightning bolt of insolence. Therefore, the portable conspiracy—whose principle characteristic was that of conspiring for the sake of conspiring—should be short-lived. Three years after Varèse's fall and Bely's breakdown—on the day of the Góngora tribute in Seville in 1927 to be precise—the Satanist Aleister Crowley, with a deliberately histrionic flourish, dissolved the secret society.

Many years after Crowley set the Shandy eagle free, I find myself in a position to reveal that the portable society exists beyond the distant horizons of its members' imagination. It was a nexus, a secret society altogether unprecedented in the history of art.

These pages will discuss those people who risked something—if not their lives, then at least their sanity—in order to create works in which the threat of the charging bull, horns lowered, was ever present. We will become acquainted with those people who paved the way for the debunking today of all those who, as Hermann Broch put it, "weren't necessarily bad writers, but were criminals."

We will meet those who paved the way for this novel about the most joyful, voluble, zany secret society that ever existed, a society of writers who seemed practically Turkish to judge by all the coffee and tobacco they got through, a society of gratuitous and outrageous heroes in the lost battle of life, lovers of writing when it becomes the most enjoyable experience possible, and also the most radical.

DARKNESS AND MAGIC

I owe to a brief conversation with Marcel Duchamp and especially to Francis Picabia's as-yet-unpublished book *Widows and Soldiers* the most valuable information regarding the key involvement of two femmes fatales in the foundation of the Shandy secret society in Port Actif.*

Picabia says that toward the end of the winter of 1924, in the city of Zurich, across the street from 1 Spiegelgasse—that is, across the street from the Cabaret Voltaire, where DADA was celebrating the happy fifth anniversary of its disappearance from the cultural scene—there was a balcony in the shape of a pygmy flute made from papaya branches, and on this balcony, under a full moon one night, a trench coat rested, inside of which fidgeted a beautiful Spanish woman with a rather horrible name, Berta Bocado, who was somewhat furtively watching the comings and goings of the old Dadaists (who, incidentally, were never aware of the Spanish woman's eyes spying on them).

---

* Yes, femmes fatales, yes. It was clear from the outset that every "bachelor machine" should incorporate into its complex workings the occasional vamp, as only thus would he function with bogus efficiency and without fear of breaking down—although, paradoxically, to "break down" was, ultimately, the fatal destiny of these machines, so admirably unproductive were they.

That night, Berta Bocado was like a camera with an open aperture: a passive, meticulous, pensive camera. She had just received a letter from her former lover—Francis Picabia—in which, after bringing her up to date, he asked her to try to become friendly with a Russian writer named Andrei Bely to ascertain whether—aside from having nervous breakdowns on enormous, towering historic rocks—he possessed ingenuity and a sense of humor. "Marcel (Duchamp) and I," the letter concluded, "are both interested to know if Bely is one of ours. The information we have suggests that he lives on the same street as you and plays chess with Tristan Tzara at sundown. He seems to function like a bachelor machine. In his best novel, *Petersburg*, the protagonist is a conspirator and, at the same time, a bachelor machine who, in a positively inspired moment, eats a bomb and feels its pleasurable tick-tock in his gut. This Bely is probably a high-grade madman. We'd like you to become acquainted with him and tell us if he has anything in common with his novel's protagonist. We await word."

It's unclear whether it was due to her being a femme fatale or simply due to her absentmindedness that Berta Bocado mistook another Russian for Bely. This Russian also lived on the Spielgasse and, from time to time, played chess with Tzara, Arp, Schwitters, and company, but he stayed home at night and wanted nothing to do with the old Dadaists. Vladimir Ilyich Ulyanov was his name and, along with a certain Krupskaya, he was biding his time in Zurich waiting for revolution to break out in his own country.

A few days later, Berta Bocado sent some totally erroneous information to Picabia, thereby creating the misunderstanding that contributed so much to the consolidation of the portable secret society: "This is certainly a strange Russian, who even when the weather is fine goes out wearing galoshes and a quilted winter coat and carrying an umbrella. He keeps the umbrella furled and his pocket watch inside a grey suede protective sleeve, and he also keeps the penknife that he uses as a pencil sharpener stowed in a case; he even seems to have his face sheathed, because he always hides it with the upturned collar of his coat. He wears dark glasses, a wool shirt, stuffs his ears with cotton wool, and when he gets in a car, he orders the driver to put the top up. In a word, this individual displays a constant tendency to create something akin to a casing that isolates him and protects him from all manner of prying eyes. I believe he even has a mania about keeping his ideas encased.... I attempted to seduce him and the best I could manage was to be allowed up to his apartment, but once inside he began to behave very oddly: he barely looked at me and only seemed interested in a number of folders that he transported convulsively from one place to another in his study. Some of these folders he moved around repeatedly, others he hid. I suppose they contained manuscripts of his novels. And I say *suppose* because all this time he insisted, over and over again, that he was not a novelist, and, horrified, I would say almost terrified, he denied ever having written anything about conspirators who swallow bombs and other such things. It was clear that he wanted me to leave as soon as possible, and this—you know me—made me angry. I called him rude, but he replied mysteriously that he wasn't rude, but simply a fan of transporting everything that seemed portable ...."

On receiving the letter, Picabia had the impression that behind the Russian's strange conduct there might be a coded message he ought to decipher. He spent days trying to uncover a meaning to the frenetic moving around of files, until Duchamp, who didn't yet know the content of the letter from Bocado, recounted a dream to him, supplying (without knowing it) the crucial clue he'd been trying so hard to find.

Duchamp said he'd dreamed four phrases, the first three constructed out of words subject to the realm of coincidence: phrases that reflected the language that might be expected of pickled chance—which, as is well known, was always his great specialty. The four phrases (except for the last) would be included years later in Andre Breton's anthology of black humor:

> *Etrangler l'etranger.*
> *Eglise, exil.*
> *Rrose Selavy et moi esquivons les*

eccymoses des Esquimaux aux mots
exquis.
C'est Bely le plus vieux du Port
Actif.

This fourth and final phrase—the only one not constructed with words subject to the realm of coincidence—acquired a magical meaning for Picabia, who believed he saw in *Port Actif* (homonym for the French word *portatif*, meaning portable) a revelation, this word cryptically linking Duchamp's dream with the Russian's message and pointing him toward Port Actif, an African village situated at the mouth of the River Niger.

After not a little difficulty, Picabia managed to convince four of his friends—Duchamp, Ferenc Szalay, Paul Morand, and Jacques Rigaut—of the absolute necessity of setting sail for the coast of Nigeria. And on July 27, 1924, they boarded a ship at Marseille bound for the African shores and a future Shandy plot. (At the time, they didn't know exactly what this plot would entail, but they had no doubt that clearly it ought to come to light, in the darkness of a continent darker than the still-opaque portable spirit.)

On arriving at Port Actif, Picabia says they felt, immediately, the alluring horror of the unknown world to which they'd traveled: "We felt transported to a new planet; I remember we disembarked at sundown, and a swarm of little black children overran the deck: they poked their shaved heads through our cabin windows, showing their beautiful eyes and bright glittering smiles; they reached out their slender hands, with palms like pink conch shells, to ask for money ... and soon we were in Port Actif's great square, four-sided and beautiful, replete with guest houses, bars, and shops. Marcel, Paul, Ferenc, and Jacques all laughed in unison when they saw there was a place called Café du Louvre. We sat there, sampling *micris*, magnificent sugar-coated coffee beans from Harar. Two Negroes came over in hope of a sale and showed us agates from Ceylon, rock crystals from Tamojal, silver rings, gazelle antlers, ostrich feathers, and Nigerian shields.... But at nightfall, once the initial astonishment at that fascinating place had passed, we began to fear that nothing of any relevance was going to happen to us there …"

They grew bored over the course of three long days on the Café du Louvre's terrace, and, in fact, none of them—not even Picabia, the one who had launched them on this escapade—was overly clear about what they were doing there. Duchamp, the most depressed of all, kept repeating, in his opinion five bachelor machines lost in an African port didn't amount to anything more than a ridiculous group of hobbled contraptions. Picabia tried to be more optimistic and, though fully aware he was deluding himself, he constantly saw—besides his friends' irritation—signs in the sky or in the square's porticoes or in the impressive miniatures that the locals sold. But not until the afternoon of the third day did Picabia think he saw a sign of real interest: a one-legged man, no less, playing a flute made from his own tibia: someone identical to Lelgoualch, a fictional character in Raymond Roussel's *Impressions of Africa*.

Darkness and magic. Picabia made the suggestion that this time, this really could be a highly revealing sign. But revealing what? Duchamp, Szalay, and company asked in unison, visibly annoyed, already very tired of Picabia's questing after free associations that might plot a course through the chaos. Then, all of a sudden, they saw a gorgeous foreign woman go by ("tall, tanned, extremely sensual, a bona fide apparition") who, crossing the square at high speed, disappeared down an alleyway and was followed by Lelgoualch and his musical tibia.

After a few moments of general stupor, Picabia reacted and, trying to work out if the others had seen the same thing he had, remarked that he'd just seen a beautiful *animated* machine. Morand said to him that, yes, indeed, a comic variation on the orange blossom had just gone by. Szalay chimed in and, attempting to guess the foreign woman's nationality, roundly confirmed that there were three sexes: men, women, and that French woman who had just furtively crossed the square. Rigaut abruptly got to his feet, beside himself, and "in love, even before meeting her, set out in pursuit of the femme fatale."

This woman turned out to be Georgia O'Keeffe, the American painter and sculptor, who was traveling along the eastern coast of Africa in the company of the poet William Carlos Williams, a good friend of Duchamp's. At the dinner following this happy encounter, she seemed enthusiastic about Picabia's talk of bachelor machines, their fictions and their other future conspiracy. Lelgoualch provided continuous musical accompaniment to everything said over dinner, to the point that his enchanted tibia would respectfully respond to the group's silence, O'Keeffe now operating as the femme fatale, already responding to the bachelor mechanism and expounding her theory as to what she understood by *extreme sexuality*: a concept intimately tied up with the functioning of the bachelor machines, which soon became one of the most characteristic Shandy traits.

Aware that the bachelor machines' most distinctive characteristic was eminently sexual, Georgia O'Keeffe asserted that they were also composites, combinations of mechanical and organic components, tied to each other in close circles, by complex bonds of pleasure and terror, ecstasy and punishment, life and death.

"Therefore, love, like energy or libido," Picabia tells us the femme fatal declared while filing her nails, "ought to be separated from its genetic purpose, which we understand as reproduction; one's own satisfaction is the only thing that should be sought. In a word, copulate for pure pleasure, never thinking about progeny or other trifles. This is what I understand by extreme sexuality."

After quoting O'Keeffe word for word, Picabia's description of the foundational soiree in Port Actif comes to an abrupt close; an enigmatic and suggestive silence—a pact—arose between the stealthy conspirators: "If up to that point we'd dragged our pasts behind us like the vaporous trails of comets, knowing precious little about our future conspiracy, Georgia's statement brought us together suddenly, in the perfect silence of stealthy conspirators, and that night there were no more words, because this struck us as the ideal tone that would allow us to slowly mold—in the most absolute and alluring of silences—the other characteristically portable traits. Everyone fell silent, understanding that there was really no need for any audible conversation, since we'd already been in conversation for a very long time (though not with expressed words). We spoke to each other silently, and our conversation was one of the most interesting imaginable; words pronounced to be heard could not have had the effect of this silence."

I have no more information on this pact of stealthy conspirators that founded Shandyism than Picabia offers in his book, but I think the facts are reliable enough for one to conclude that, thanks to the definition of extreme sexuality by a femme fatale, the birth of the portables' world became reality: a universe that was born of mistakes and coincidences. Of mistakes, such as Berta Bocado's confusing one Russian for another. And of coincidences, such as the encounter with Georgia O'Keeffe, leading to the expulsion of maternity from the Shandy language.

All seems to indicate, then, that the influence of femmes fatales on the portable world brought about the birth of the secret society. But, as is well known, to be born is to begin to die. That the femmes fatales installed themselves in the Shandy bachelor machines did not exempt the latter from irreparable future breakdowns, since, at the very moment they became aware they were alive and portable, they embraced Death, which explains both the immediate appearance of the word suicide on their horizon and the fact that one of those who dined in Port Actif—specifically the one who had fallen in love with the femme fatale—took charge there and then of the fate of one of the portable "offices," *the General Suicide Agency.*

HOTEL SUICIDES

It seems to be historically constant that among founding members of secret societies, there is always one who likes to contradict the rest. In the Shandy's case, all of those who dined in Port Actif were great lovers of life except for Rigaut, who declared himself, from the outset, on the side of death ("*Vous êtes tous de poètes et moi je suis du côte de la mort*"), more concretely of suicide, a word that would not be banished from the Shandy's language until the day Rigaut—after vacillating for two years—committed suicide in an opulent hotel in the city of Palermo.

He took so long to come to this decision that he had time to witness the famous wave of youthful suicides in Paris in 1924, a trend sternly criticized by some of those who'd dined in Port Actif: "This whole thing of taking one's life nowadays," wrote Szalay, "seems to be the exclusive domain of willfully moronic youths, and the most youthful and moronic of all—or, at least, the one closest to us—is our impetuous Rigaut; something will have to be done about extreme youth and suicide, two words that currently seem intertwined and that are very much at odds with the portable spirit." And Paul Morand, with clear reference to his friend Rigaut, concluded a lecture in Reims with these words: "Sirs, suicide is ridiculous. If one wishes to take one's life it ought to be done in a timely manner, that is, when one is still a child; doing it any later is slightly ridiculous, for one can no longer be timid after the age of seven."

Rigaut paid scant attention to his friends' words: since coming back from Africa, suicide had become his one and only sacrament. He'd taken his first steps toward this definitive gesture in Port Actif. Without telling anyone, he walked off into the jungle and disappeared into a dark night of large trees. There, surrounded by the lush silence of the leaves, he invented the pretext of being hopelessly in love with Georgia O'Keeffe, as this would make suicide all the more tempting. He was sure his beloved would reject him outright, which, as it turned out, was quite right. But, as I've said, this didn't prevent him from taking two more years to commit suicide.

It is also the case that, feeling enormously wretched and suicidal brought Rigaut's sense of humor back, as can clearly be seen in this announcement, which, on returning from Port Actif, he drew up in Paris, attempting to publicize his General Suicide Agency (a singular office in the history of portable literature):

"Among other benefits, the GSA at last offers a reputable means of passing away, death being the least excusable of moral failings. That is why we have organized an Express burial service: including a banquet, a farewell to friends and relations, photograph (or death mask if preferred), distribution of effects, suicide, placement of body in coffin, religious ceremony (optional), transport of body to the ceremony. The GSA pledges to carry out the last wishes of its esteemed clients."

Two months after the publication of this advertisement, Rigaut abruptly left his suicide office and set sail for America. His fondness for wistful comedies led him to the door of none other than William Carlos Williams (whom he supposed was O'Keeffe's lover), where he tried to show his profound desperation as a jilted lover.

We have some very interesting details from his ocean voyage, during which he struck up a friendship with an elegant passenger, the photographer Man Ray, who years later would go on to recount the whole thing unsparingly in an amusing book called *Travels with Rita Malú*. Rigaut would be described as a pitiful and histrionic gentleman, pandering to a desperation that, ultimately, even he didn't believe in, as his sense of humor gave him away on several occasions. For example, when Rigaut disembarked in New York, he felt compelled to publish this ad in the local press:

> Poor, mediocre youth, 21 years old, clean hands, seeks matrimony with woman: 24 cylinders, healthy, eroto-maniac, or fluent in Annamese, if possible surnamed O'Keeffe. Contact Jacques Rigaut, 73 Boulevard de Mont-parnasse, Paris. No permanent address in New York.

Once the ad was placed, he made his way to the house of William Carlos Williams, who, on opening the door and seeing the future suicide's unhinged and grotesque countenance, couldn't hold back his laughter. There Rigaut stood, bearing a bouquet of orchids, wearing pale makeup and the expression of a victim of an amo-rous, heart-piercing fever. This spectacle was ripe for a photograph, and Man Ray, who had accompanied Rigaut to the house, didn't hesitate. His snapshot, when it circulated among the early Shandies, confirmed that there was no place in their secret society for this un-wittingly ridiculous or put-on desperation of extreme youthfulness.

This meeting in a New Jersey doorway was also the start of a friendship between the North American poet and Man Ray. The latter (already friends with Duchamp) would in turn initiate a long lasting relationship with O'Keeffe and the exquisite Shandies. O'Keeffe, on her return from Port Actif, had patiently been enlisting from among the most select artists in New York, a city that, thanks to the nascent portable furor, was putting aside its provincialism.

Those who stood out among Georgia O'Keeffe's friends were Walter Arensberg, Pola Negri, Prince Mdivani, Skip Canell, and Rob-ert Johnson. This last seemed to Man Ray to be "marked by traces of a hollowing out, a rift, and the foreshadowing of death." And he was clearly a very odd character.

For a long time, Johnson had been showing up to all engagements carrying a very light briefcase, which everyone thought contained his paintings in miniature, until it was discovered that it was a picnic case containing a soup tureen, four trays, twelve dishes, six glasses, and a baroque silver teapot.

But the oddest thing about Johnson was that, though reminiscent of Rigaut in certain ways, unlike him, he seemed in an enormous hurry to leave this world. On meeting him, Rigaut felt surprised, ashamed, and extremely unsettled in the face of a far more determined suicide. "Take a good look at me tonight," Johnson said, "because I doubt you'll see me again. In a few hours, I'll no longer exist." And indeed, soon after returning home, Johnson decided to finish the task he'd started long ago: consisting of a delicate piece of silversmithery. Johnson polished the handle of his baroque silver teapot until it was perfectly rounded and used it as a projectile with which to blow out his brains.

What Johnson could never have imagined was that his death transformed him into a kind of Werther in New York; the city— from one day to the next, in imitation of Paris—began to teem with suicidal youths. Dazzled by that death by baroque silver teapot, they flung themselves from suspension bridges, but not before writing droll letters to judges outlining the many reasons for giving up this life.

One of these suicidal youths, the brother of the sculptor Gaudier-Brezska, was thoughtful enough to dedicate the following admirable poem to his judge: "Tomorrow, the end. / The end, tomorrow. / Until tomorrow, the end. / The end, tomorrow. / To the end, tomorrow."

The wave of suicides was so huge that Skip Canell, a close friend of Johnson's, asked Rigaut—since he was a recognized authority on the subject of suicides—to publish without delay a call to young people, urging them to desist from such suicidal inclinations. So it was that, at the end of December, 1924, a letter to the editor appeared in the pages of *The New York Times*, written by Jacques Rigaut.

> There's nothing to live for, nor is there anything to die for.
> I would like, Mr. Editor, for this letter to make clear to the
> youth of your city that the only way to show disdain for
> life is to accept it. Life isn't worth the trouble it takes to
> leave it.... Suicide is very comfortable, too comfortable:

I haven't committed suicide. I wouldn't want to leave regretting not having taken with me the Statue of Liberty, or love, or the United States. I send my most energetic protest against this absurd wave of suspension-bridge suicides. Youth of New York: choose sumptuous hotels if you want to leave this life. Some hotels are, frankly, rather literary. (After all, the world of letters rests in the hotels of the imagination.) In Europe they've known this for a long time and consider suicides elegant only if they happen in places like the Ritz.

This letter led to an outrageous increase in the number of suicides as well as letters to judges (the opposite effect to what Skip Canell had hoped for). A letter written by Canell's most beloved nephew is famous: "Your Honor, I'm pleased to tell you that I've chosen to commit suicide on the day when I'm due to inherit a large fortune from my uncle."

According to Man Ray, Jacques Rigaut's letter helped the Shandies uncover a new characteristic: a radical rejection of any idea of suicide as a benighted romantic tic. "Rigaut's text," he wrote, "made clear that, of all of us, he was the only one who believed in suicide. The rest of us were sure that a hydroplane, for example, was a million times more attractive than the wind-blown mane, the suicidal indigestion, of Heinrich von Kleist beside the green bay of the Wannsee."

Out of the blue, one of the New York suicides had a profound effect on Rigaut. His best friend in the city, a concierge at the Ritz, hanged himself in the hotel lobby. Downcast and ashamed, Rigaut took his briefcase and hurried back to Paris, where he became hefty and his shadow (errant and voluminous) wandered the streets of Montmartre; he tried desperately to delay a suicide that seemed to him increasingly inevitable. He moved from one hotel to the next, accompanied by a beautiful black woman, Carla Orengo, and dragging a heavy trunk that was, actually, a writing bureau with two shelves for huge tomes, three drawers for documents, a compartment for the typewriter, and a folding table. Man Ray thinks that the weight of this trunk, which Rigaut realized wasn't portable, could have been one of the reasons why he made up his mind, finally, to commit suicide, choosing the Grand Hotel in the city of Palermo as the place to do it.*

It was at the end of 1926 that Rigaut installed himself in this hotel, having taken measures to ensure he'd never return to Paris. In the trunk's drawers were all manner of barbiturates, which he constantly ingested, trying to kill himself, plunging into a great orgy of pills as though he'd now taken a liking to death, which previously he'd so feared.

The morning he was supposed to leave his hotel to go to Kreuzlingen for a detoxification cure, he was found dead. In spite of his extreme weakness, he'd dragged himself and his mattress to the door adjoining Carla Orengo's room. This door had always been open, but was found locked with a key. (One final gesture on a mattress, as grotesque as it was indecipherable.)

Man Ray says that when the news arrived in Paris the Shandies thought that thereafter, in the bosom of the secret society, they ought to avoid other capricious suicides and disseminated an array of texts about the perfection of Rigaut's suicide. They thought that if they said this one was impossible to improve upon, future portables would discard the idea of trying to better Rigaut. Blaise Cendrars, for example, wrote: "In the hotel in Palermo, the key, the bolt, and that closed door formed—in that moment and indubitably forever—an enigmatic triangle: both offering and denying us Rigaut's deed. In any case, an insuperable suicide. My friends, I recommend not at-

---

* The exact name is *Grand Hotel et des Palmes*. Following Rigaut's suicide, it became a pilgrimage site for anyone in possession of the portable secret. It can be visited nowadays and is well worth the trip—it has other points of historical interest such as being a clear reflection of Sicily's splendor and misery during its transition from the House of Savoy to the Republic. I ought finally to sound a note of caution: the hotel is run by a group of academic elephants, who only show visitors the room where Wagner once spent the night, making out that Rigaut was never there.

tempting to better it, for that would be an impossible task, and there would be nothing worse than killing yourself and making a fool of yourself, and, to top it all off, not even knowing you'd done that."

In the opinion of Maurice Blanchot—in *Faux Pas*, he briefly but lucidly analyzed the portable phenomenon—the proliferation of texts that sought to eradicate suicide weren't attempts to convince others, but rather the authors themselves. Blanchot was very likely correct in a number of cases. For example, in the poem Prince Mdivani wrote in a stationary submarine, "And the Mattress?," his quill must have trembled, or he was going insane, or, simply, he was in a deep panic at feeling tempted by suicide. Whatever it was, he wrote these inept verses dedicated to Rigaut's barbiturates: "Phanodorme, Variane, Rutonai. Hipalène, Acetile, Somnothai. Neurinase, Veronin, Goodbye." Paul Morand, never less than witty, construed this poem as "something truly brilliant, as it has revealed to me the possibility of realizing suicide in the process of writing."

To realize suicide in the process of writing. What came into the world as an ironic comment ended up becoming a principle agreed upon by all members of the secret society. It was very clear, from then on, that suicide could only be realizable on paper. Antonin Artaud, for example, responded in this way to a surrealist inquiry, where those interrogated had to give their opinion on the subject of taking one's life: "But what would you say to an anterior suicide, one which made you retrace your steps, not to the side of death, but *to the other side of existence*. This is the only suicide that would have value for me. I have no appetite for death, but I have an appetite for not existing, for never having fallen into this interlude of imbecilities, abdications, renunciations, and obtuse encounters ..."

Although initially, as we've seen, each Shandy with his drama was to understand that he'd come down on the side of death, soon it would become clear that suicide was not a solution, but nor was it nothing. It could only be realized in the same space as writing: whether, as we'll see, by repeating the most radical silence, or indeed by transforming oneself into a literary character, or by betraying language itself, or by drinking liquor strong as molten metal, or by

21

steering off into trompe l'œil or optical illusions, or certain kinds of smoke and mirrors. These were portable solutions to suit all tastes, to put aside this language of death that, two years before, wandering around Montmartre, carrying a trunk and some sort of bundle, Rigaut had discovered. He had done so deep in impressions of Africa (those of Port Actif), where, it seems, the whole thing began.

THE PARTY IN VIENNA

"I had actually been invited."
—F. Scott Fitzgerald, *The Great Gatsby*

At the beginning of 1925, the musician George Antheil appeared on the Shandy scene brimming with energy. With his announcement of Nicotechnica—a science invented by Antheil himself consisting of a fount of knowledge that categorically disproved the existence of the thriving secret society—he sowed seeds of uncertainty, as well as a certain despondency, among the portables. After that, amidst the confusion he had generated, Antheil published a curious tract that had the effect of revitalizing the Shandies, propelling them into a kind of highly creative secret euphoria with some extraordinary results, including a first-rate essay by the ill-fated Anthony Typhon in which he praised Despondency as an inexhaustible source of new and stimulating sensations.*

It's worth noting that Typhon's own despondency was so great, he even eliminated the *h*'s from his first and last names. At the same time, he proposed George Antheil be given a medal, which led to

---

* *Nicotechnica: A Denial.* Since this isn't the most interesting of texts, I didn't refer to it in the Essential Bibliography at the end of this *Brief History*. A version does exist in Spanish, published by Janés (Barcelona, 1951), in a bungled translation by Venancio Ramos; a frenzied chapter in praise of tobacco is of some interest.

Typhon's immediate expulsion from the group, since if there was anything the Shandies to a man found appalling, it was insignia, medals, or honors of any kind.

Typhon fled to Martinique; there, he set up a stationery shop in a village where they spoke a strange local variant of Creole and no French and barely wrote at all. The little paper they did use, they bought from a dealer in the nearby municipality of Saint-Joseph, in the middle of the island. He soon bankrupted the business buying his own merchandise. He'd occasionally write letters to Antheil begging forgiveness in an extraordinarily sincere tone that was nevertheless always belied by his unswerving inclusion at the end of the missive, each and every time, of the same postscript: "I've recently been working on perfecting the game of Love, availing myself of coal tar," and then he'd cynically turn his signature (Typ(h)on) into a drawing of an insignia or medal.

George Antheil—who years later would go on to compose the controversial *Ballet Mécanique* (a Shandy musical par excellence)—became accustomed to receiving Typhon's letters and giving them no more than a minute of his time, now that the portable conspiracy required his attention twenty-four hours a day. It was Antheil, for instance, who found the ideal place for the group's first secret meetings: Shakespeare & Company, the bookshop situated at number 12, Rue de l'Odéon, and run by Sylvia Beach.

George Antheil lived in the two-room apartment above the bookshop and often entered through the window. Shandily, he would scale the front of the building. Sylvia Beach, in her mediocre memoirs, says that the portables met in the bookshop every Friday, occasionally admitting some new member. Antheil was master of ceremonies. Apparently, he was also the inventor of the method for finding portable artists on the streets of Paris. For a year Antheil strolled the terraces of Montparnasse and Saint Germain, in perfect silence, making conspiratorial gestures, and distributing the alphabet manual for the deaf. Along with the alphabet, there were some instructions, incomprehensible at first sight: twelve phrases that only made sense when read vertically and the first letter of each phrase spelled out the following address: SEPT RUE ODÉON.

Apart from that, the first of the phrases, translated to Spanish (Si Hablas Alto Nunca Digas Yo), would have been of interest should anyone discover the word spelled out by its capital letters:

That is: SHANDY.

It's important to bear in mind that more than referring to the book by Laurence Sterne, the word shandy invokes alcohol. Shandy is commonly drunk in London—a mixture of beer and either fizzy lemonade or ginger beer—and a pint of shandy with ice is thirst quenching in the summertime.

So, the address of a house on Rue de l'Odéon, and the word shandy. If anyone worked this out they'd understand that, by mysterious means, they were being invited to a house to drink shandy. And that person would soon go and have a look around the vicinity of number 7, Rue de l'Odéon. There, Blaise Cendrars would ask him the simple question: "Are you deaf?" "Yes," he'd generally answer. Blaise Cendrars would point him in the direction of Sylvia Beach's bookshop and, departing at an unmistakably conspiratorial (leisurely) pace, would say: "As you can see, it's not number 7 but number 12. Friday, at eight o'clock, we'll be expecting you."*

Among the Shandies that Antheil and Cendrars brought in off the street Valery Larbaud stood out from the beginning as the heart and soul of the first world deaf conference held at Shakespeare and Company. Valery Larbaud was the portable artist par excellence. His sexuality was extreme, and he was vehemently opposed to any idea of suicide. Additionally, his fraught coexistence with doppelgängers was outstanding, as was his sympathy for negritude, his perfect functioning as a "bachelor machine," his disinterest in grand statements, his cultivation of the art of insolence, and his passion for traveling with a small suitcase containing almost weightless versions of his work.

Clearly, an out-and-out Shandy. He was your typical learned and worldly gentleman, who didn't turn up his nose at friendships, aspired to an international culture, a world of broad horizons and

* Seven, twelve, and eight add up to twenty-seven, which, as we'll see, was the Shandy number par excellence.

lofty origins: a splendid ideal marking the period between the wars. He apparently showed a precocious vocation for travel: he loved the smell of leather in trains and the successive landscape, which appeared motionless, yet would still pass by. He was only five years old when he crossed a border for the first time—the one between France and Switzerland—and he was surprised not to see that red and lilac line one sees on maps (which he had scrutinized so attentively, his first game).

He was, like any good portable, also enthusiastic about miniature things. In her memoirs, Sylvia Beach tells us Larbaud had an enormous army of toy soldiers and complained that they were beginning to crowd him out of his rooms, but he made no effort to control them. "The soldiers perhaps accounted for another obsession of his—his colors. They were blue, yellow, and white, and so were his cufflinks and his ties. His colors flew from the roof of his country house whenever he was in it (which was not often, since he preferred to be in Paris or traveling about)."

Larbaud was also a traveler of words: "I fixate on winding clocks to make sure they tell the right time, putting things where they belong, polishing those things that have gotten tarnished, bringing to light things relegated to the shadows, mending and cleaning old toys from forgotten civilizations in people's lofts ..." It was in one such loft that Larbaud decided on the phrase that came to be used to swear in new members to the secret society, a definition from *Tristram Shandy*: "Gravity: a mysterious carriage of the body to cover the defects of the mind."

And if we add to all this his passion for discovering unexplored, portablist literary territories (Savinio, Littbarski, Gómez de la Serna, Stephan Zenith, and a very youthful Borges were among those he invited to join the secret society), we get a rough picture of this writer whose figure (although outshone in this century's cultural panorama) is fundamental to understanding how portable literature consolidated itself. It was Larbaud, in fact, who organized the Shandy party in Vienna, in March, 1925.

A month before, Larbaud went to scout out the city as a possible location for a party; having to be top secret, it called for certain special conditions. For the illustrious traveler arriving in Vienna at that time, the most important—and the gravest—man then living there was Karl Kraus. Nobody had the slightest doubt about that. Here was a writer who went on the offensive against everything substandard, everything rotten. He edited a review to which he, and he alone, contributed. Everything submitted by other people struck him as inopportune. For the review, he never accepted invitations to collaborate on projects, and he didn't answer letters. Every word, every syllable published in *Die Fackel* was written by him. Every claim he made was rigorously correct. Never since has there been such scrupulousness in literature. He concerned himself—scrupulously—with each and every comma. Anyone who wanted to uncover any kind of erratum in *Die Fackel* could spend entire weeks torturing himself in search of just one. Best simply not to try.

But it so happened that a little before Larbaud's arrival in Vienna, an injudicious young writer named Werner Littbarski set out to find that elusive erratum, and with the help of his black Brazilian servant Virgil, after several sleepless days and nights, he found it. Littbarski had a champagne celebration, just him and Virgil, but he imagined a multitude of friends visiting, whose voices and cries he imitated, making a considerable din, once again upsetting the neighbors, who for a long time had known this to be Littbarski's great specialty: throwing make-believe mass parties in his apartment.

In the days following the triumphant discovery of the erratum, Littbarski, usings his father's old printing press to publish an anti-Krausian review entitled *Ich Vermute*, went some way to reinforcing his neighbors' image of him as a madman.* The review's one and only edition contained twenty-four pages written entirely by Littbarski, except for one opinion piece by Virgil, which opened as follows: "Today I have ceased to hold any kind of opinion about

---

* A facsimile copy, under the dubiously translated title *Supongo* (*I Suppose*) was included in *Papeles de Son Armadans*, CCLXXI (Palma de Mallorca, October 1979).

anything." Littbarski's review featured insults against Kraus, jokes of questionable taste, ads for strong liquor, Indian postcards, mysterious "safe-conduct passes," pornographic tales, drawings of elephant tusks, comic vignettes with Kraus's grandmother as the main character. In short, it was an obscene display of boundless aggression.

All Vienna took pity on Littbarski; if it had been said before that he was mad because he threw make-believe parties, now, to top it off, he was trying to make a laughing stock of Karl Kraus, which could only upset people and discredit him further socially, and intellectually.

But on his mission as secret Shandy ambassador, Valery Larbaud arrived in Vienna and saw in Littbarksi the ideal host for this international party. (The party had to happen away from Paris and Shandyism's other nerve centers, and furthermore, it mustn't draw the attention of citizens who weren't part of the secret portable movement.)

Larbaud saw right away that one of Littbarski's make-believe parties could conceal an actual party, full of conspirators from around the world. Their presence in Vienna would go perfectly unnoticed if they knew to disappear in the dawn mist, at the right moment.

Convinced that this energy of Littbarski's—so unproductive, so crazy and portable—could easily be channeled in the direction of the luxurious and useless Shandy planet, Larbaud sent him a letter. Though mostly incoherent, the letter did include a secret "key" that would give birth to new friendships and connect the members of a small, clandestine society that imperceptibly, implacably, was expanding.

"I understand, my friend," Littbarski wrote back. "I understand. And please be aware that your key is of interest to me. You are opening the door to one of those pavilions that, since I was a child, has undergone fewer changes than other kinds of quarters. But that isn't the only reason I still feel attached to them: it's the solace, too, emanating from the fact that they are uninhabitable for anyone waiting to establish himself permanently somewhere. The truth is that anyone struggling to establish a firm foothold in the world could never inhabit them. The possibility of dwelling in these places is limited. Vienna is born in them, and I was born in Vienna, to see them reborn.

PS: Indeed, I am single, and, yes, my servant is black."

It seemed to Larbaud that Littbarski had played with two meanings of the word lodge. The houses in Vienna also had glass-domed pavilions outside that were used for household clutter. He also had meant to indicate that he understood perfectly that the offer of a "key" would bring him into contact with portable literature, that is, with a non-existent literature, seeing as none of the Shandies knew what it consisted of (though paradoxically this was what made it possible). It was a literature to whose rhythm the members of the secret society danced, conspiring for the sake of—and on the basis of—nothing.

According to what I know about the preparations for the party in Vienna—and the fact is, I know very little, the only place I've found reference to them is in Miriam Cendrars's *Inédits secrets*—one of these typically Viennese lodges provided the setting for Littbarski and Larbaud's first encounter: one in which Littbarski decided, for the first time in years, to tell anyone about an odd novel he was writing entitled *A Bachelor Opens Fire* (a bibliographical rarity nowadays). This was a text he'd been working on since time immemorial, ever since he'd had the use of reason, to be precise. What made the novel so odd wasn't how long he'd invested in it but rather the fact that he himself thought he'd only written one decent page in all that time: a miserable wine-soaked little sheet of paper that he showed to Larbaud. Girding himself with patience, Larbaud read it:

"Feeling bored, little Hermann stood looking out the window of the concierge's office managed by his parents. A child he'd never seen before came and stood in front of him, and in a gesture Hermann found brazen and defiant, the child joyfully emptied a whole bottle of French champagne onto the sidewalk. Hermann would never forgive the boy."

When, out of sheer courtesy, Larbaud inquired about the novel's plot, Littbarski gave the following answer: "It's the story of Hermann, a man who gratuitously wastes his life despising a person, and that person's crime, if he'd ever committed one, was to pour away a bottle of champagne as a child. Hermann gives himself body and soul to embittering his enemy's life, even avoiding marriage so as not to waste a single minute on trivialities, anything other than the relentless persecution of that French-champagne squanderer. From time to time, Hermann snipes at the other's life, that is to say, he makes certain opportune incursions (he steals his enemy's wife, lodges complaints against his business, chops his mother up into small pieces, kills his dog, sets fire to his house, etc.), brief but sharp shots fired by the bachelor from vantages where the despised man can't spot him. The poor despised man goes through his life in the novel confused and frightened because even the weight of the years can't slow the hate directed at him by a stranger of whom the only thing he knows is that, operating invisibly and out of reach, he dedicates himself with peculiar obstinacy (and considerable success) to embittering his life."

When he finished, Larbaud asked him what Karl Kraus had done when they were children to provoke such hatred. The question didn't surprise Littbarski, who answered: "He poured champagne over my powers of reason. Fair grounds, wouldn't you say?" Larbaud, choosing to believe that what he'd just heard was a metaphor, moved on to what he was actually interested in, proposing they organize a party that would bring together in Vienna the secret society's most incisive members. "They're coming from far and wide," said Larbaud, "and the only real requisite is that they pass unnoticed by the citizens of Vienna." That said, he asked if they might swap suitcases; an enigmatic petition, to which Littbarski said yes. Even Miriam Cendrars found it difficult to explain: "Whenever he spoke to me about the preparations for the party, Larbaud would go quiet at this point. It made him uncomfortable and anxious to speak about this swapping of the suitcases. He never wanted to explain it to me. Perhaps—if anyone decides to research deeply into the secret society's unknown history and to write a book about it—I may come to understand the mystery of the swapping of the suitcases.

I'm confident it will happen, and I'll see the day. Until then, without any further information, I'll stick to my suspicion that Larbaud's silence can be explained by the fact there was something very important in the suitcases."

I'm sorry for Miriam Cendrars, but I've found it impossible to ascertain the truth about the Vienna suitcase swap. Still, I'd like to remind Ms. Cendrars that the Shandies, never thinking themselves important, didn't carry things of importance in their light luggage, only miniature works, every single one of which (without exception), reflected their utter disdain for what's considered important. I wouldn't want anyone to think my words here are a diversionary tactic to cover up the fact that I've failed in my research. It's just that I believe the suitcase matter is neither an enigma, nor particularly important; in fact, I don't even think this history of the portable literature is.

As I was saying, after the suitcase swap, Littbarski was enthusiastic at the prospect of the party, explaining that a number of things about his apartment allowed for evacuation within minutes if circumstances required. A back door was camouflaged by centuries of ivy growth and totally unknown to his neighbors. What could be better? Larbaud must have thought. Right then and there, they agreed on a date for the party, on March 27th, 1925. "An explosion of stellar conversations and the cherries of vagabond greetings," one of their helpers, Vicente Huidobro, said. In his diary, we find the following sketch:

"Under a full moon in Vienna one night, when everything is as everything is beheld. An astrological and ephemeral house, falling from universe to universe. All the portable mob's bigwigs were there. Explosion of disguises, artifices and Viennese gondolas. An absolute explosion of stellar conversations and the cherries of vagabond greetings. Drinks and distant diamonds. The planets were coming to fruition in the firmament, and our eyes beheld the essence of birds, the water lilies' beyond, the hereafter of butterflies. The vessel of our secrets navigated the stealthy, starry nocturne. And Paris was this kaleidoscope: Duchamp, Scott Fitzgerald, Dalí,

Man Ray, Larbaud, and Céline. Oh! and George Antheil. Peru was pure swordplay: César Vallejo. The waiter: black Virgil. Snow of yore swirled over the New York lodge: marvelous Georgia O'Keeffe, Pola Negri, Skip Canell, and Stephan Zenith. Spain, or Juan Gris, and Rita Malú, recently hitched in Havana. Prince Mdivani in the mist and Gustav Meyrink in the Bohemian cut crystal. Savinio's veils in the Eternal City, and Tristan Tzara with poisoned bear honey in Zurich. Berta Bocado or her silk needle. Walter Benjamin and/or the internal vertigo of Gombrowicz, and the rainbow of the piano-playing backsides of the irate neighbors. Huidobro wasn't there."

Actually it was Picabia who wasn't there, and who, paradoxically, has written most about the Viennese party. Though he doesn't give any of the gathering's names, he says they were exactly twenty-seven in number, and then he informs us that twenty-seven was the Shandy number par excellence: "Stephan Zenith turned twenty-seven that March 27th in Vienna. And twenty-seven is also the number of years Rita Malú had been confined in a remote Somalian asylum. It was the intervention of the generation of Spanish poets of '27 that put paid to the portables' stellar voyage. I was married one December 27th. The painting by Paul Klee dedicated to the number twenty-seven admirably encapsulates the light and shadow of the secret society; anyone can go see it at the home of Countess Van-sept, who lives at number 27 on a Paris street and has twenty-seven grandchildren, etc ..."

Picabia's account of the party is especially interesting for its description of the soiree's final few minutes, in which we find an image of F. Scott Fitzgerald far removed from the one we've had of him until now as an alcoholic: "We had struck up a stupendous conversation vis-à-vis our artistic tastes and all agreed that we were in favor of brevity when it came to literature, that we'd rather even the most brilliant books didn't go on too long. We suddenly saw a glint in Scott's eye. Some kind of rare elation seemed to have taken hold of him. He seemed in a feverish state and was struggling to talk about literature. The monocle he'd taken from Tzara kept falling off, and the movement he made to put it back on was becoming more and more strained. Intrigued, we decided to watch him more closely, and it was then that we saw a small gold box at his side. He was constantly leaning down over it on the pretext that he had a cold. We realized he'd swapped literature for winter sports, that is, his nose was sliding across the white snow of the purest cocaine."

Meanwhile, the neighbors (certain by now that such an uproar couldn't, on this occasion, be made by just one man) called the police. Valery Larbaud informed Littbarski of his desire to publish an annotated edition of his pathetic wine-soaked little quarto, which was roundly cheered by the whole gathering, especially black Virgil, who, immersed in an extraordinary euphoria (confirmation that all the waiters were drunk), took up his master's old sawn-off shotgun and, by way of a one-gun salute, put four holes in the roof. All the portables took flight, all except Scott Fitzgerald, who stayed on and kept Littbarski company (for his part, he was visibly shaken by his servant's behavior).

Scott Fitzgerald lowered himself unhurriedly onto a sofa and when the neighbors and police showed up, he lit a Virginia cigar. Pretending to be playing chess with his host, among the broken glasses, he said in an extraordinarily elated tone:

"I had actually been invited."

And he didn't hesitate to transfer the phrase, word for word, into the novel he was writing at the time.

LABYRINTH OF ODRADEKS

The memory is so intense that I always remember it in the present tense: Sitting on the terrace of a café in Portbou, watching the last summer evening of 1966 draw to a close, Marcel Duchamp is telling me about the party in Vienna, black Virgil's gunshots and the Shandy society, of whose existence I've known nothing about until this point. The café is a short distance from the guesthouse in which, twenty-seven years before, Walter Benjamin was compelled to commit suicide.

Drinking Pastis, Marcel Duchamp tells me the moving story of the involuntary suicide and explains that the portable history would have gone off quite differently had it not been for Walter Benjamin's providential intervention on the murky dawn the Shandies, fleeing Littbarski's apartment, began to scatter, totally disoriented. They fled through a ghostly Vienna in which, suddenly, a chunk of wall fell to the ground, looking like a man walking along, and the ice around them turned into the shapes of rigid faces.

In those moments of panic and dispersal, seeing the Shandies fleeing in all different directions, and knowing it would be extremely difficult to regroup, Benjamin managed to come up with an instruction that would bring them all back together in the city of Prague; he recommended they take rooms at guesthouses in Gustav Meyrink's neighborhood and that they should try, through fortuitous street encounters, to make contact again.

None of the Shandies forgot his instructions, understanding immediately during their terrified flight, and this meant that the Shandy journey could carry on: a journey that sought no goal, no fixed object, and that was clearly futile. They were like medieval pilgrims for whom the journey was all; arriving in Canterbury, Jerusalem, or Santiago de Compostela mattered little. They traveled merely so they could tell each other stories.

The north wind picks up, sending us inside the café, where I open a bottle of champagne; the cork, after violently crashing against the ceiling, bounces off the top of a piece of furniture and comes to rest in perfect equilibrium on the top of a curtain rail. All the customers are dumbfounded at this, and the landlord forbids anyone from touching the cork, as he wants to show it to all his clientele. Smiling, Duchamp says this cork is my Odradek. It's the first time I've ever heard the word, and I ask what it means. In a tone of strict confidence, Duchamp introduces me to one of Shandyism's most enigmatic aspects: the existence of certain dark occupants lodged within each of the portables' inner labyrinths.

Apparently, it was in the infinite labyrinth of the city of Prague that the dark occupants, also known as Odradeks, began to show themselves. Due to their fraught coexistence with doppelgängers, each of the Shandies had one of these dark occupants lodged within them—up until that point they'd been discreet companions for the most part, but in Prague they began to turn demanding and take assorted forms, sometimes human.

Alone or in pairs, the portables began arriving in Prague. And on taking rooms at guesthouses in the Jewish quarter, they began to feel the increasingly active presence of the dark occupants, along with the anguished certainty that their most authentic and intimate selves were being torn away, premeditatedly and against their will, merely so the ghostly figures could take plastic form.

Skip Canell speaks in his memoirs about his Odradek, who turned out to be nothing less than a sword swallower: "Not long after arriving in Prague, in a guesthouse in the city center, I was in my room, sitting at the desk I'd cobbled together, when I heard the door open. I turned, thinking some colleague of mine must have found out where I was, and saw my self coming into the room, approaching and sitting at the desk facing me, propping his head in his hand and beginning to dictate what I was writing. We spent a number of hours like that, until, finally, I managed to bring myself to ask him who he was. He was a sword swallower, he said, and a devotee of the dagger. We had dinner in the guesthouse dining room, where something genuinely astonishing took place: the poor sword swallower absentmindedly gulped down a fork, and I had to take him to a clinic, where, after a spectacular operation, a doctor removed it. I've never seen the Odradek again, but I have the sensation that he is swirling around me and might at any moment reappear."

In another guesthouse in Prague's Jewish quarter, the Spanish painter Juan Gris wrote down the following in a music notation book: "I find myself profoundly unsettled, as I wait to run into one of my friends here in the city of Prague. In the old houses of this neighborhood I feel spectral movements. I have come to understand, to my astonishment, who the hidden rulers of the alleyway are where I'm staying. Strange characters live here, similar to shadows: beings not of woman born, whose ways of thinking and acting are pieced together from random fragments. When they pass through my spirit, I feel more inclined than ever to believe that dreams have an abode all their own; I think they inhabit or hide inside dark truths latent in my soul, when I'm awake, like the vivid impressions of brightly colored tales."

When Stephan Zenith arrived in Prague, he also discovered that he was giving lodging to a dark occupant, whose form, in this case, wasn't exactly human. Terrified, he decided to leave the city though not before leaving the following illuminating note to Witold Gombrowicz, with whom he'd been sharing a room:

"I'm leaving, because I am afraid of myself, and what is certain is that Prague is making a powerful contribution to this. Bid farewell to our colleagues on my behalf should you manage to run into them, and tell them larger forces have compelled me to go back to New York. I'd like them to know I had a wonderful time at the party, except for when that guy went crazy with the gun. As I say, I'm leaving because I'm afraid of myself, now that I believe something akin to a spool of black thread is lodged within me—and sometimes without. It tries to make me say things I neither think nor will ever think. The spool is flat and star-shaped; in fact, it seems covered in threads: old threads, of course—interwoven, knotted together—but also other kinds of threads that are other colors, also interwoven and knotted together.

"But it isn't simply a spool; a small pole sticks straight up out of the center of the star, and another attaches to this at a right angle. With this latter pole on one side, and one of the beams of the star on the other, the ensemble manages to stay upright, as though standing on two limbs. Often, when one goes out of the guesthouse door and finds it leaning there in the stairwell, one feels the urge to talk to it. One naturally addresses it with simple questions, treating it rather like a child (perhaps because it is small).

"And what's *your* name?"

"Odradek," it says.

"And where do you live?"

"Domicile unknown," it says, laughing; the laughter, of course, is of someone who has no lungs. It sounds more or less like the whispering of fallen leaves.... I'm frightened, Witold, and that's why I'm leaving. Perhaps, away from Prague, I'll manage to shake off my Odradek."

On the basis of this text, the dark occupants quickly came to be termed *Odradeks* in the Shandy lexicon. And being in Prague too, George Antheil and Hermann Kromberg echoed Zenith's text, speaking frankly of Odradeks, referring to their respective dark occupants. In George Antheil's case, the Odradek wasn't a spool but a pin stuck in a ribbon, while for Hermann Kromberg, it wasn't a tiny object but became a spectral figure again.

"Here in Prague," wrote Antheil, "while running into my colleagues again, I have come to understand that I only experience minor sensations—those associated with very small things—intensely. My love of futility is the reason why. Perhaps my scrupulous attention to detail. But I do rather think—I'm not sure, I never analyze such things—that it's because minimal things, having absolutely no social or practical importance, do have, merely due to this absence, absolute independence from unclean associations with reality. Minimal things—and my Odradek is one—always feel unreal to me. These useless things are beautiful, because they're less real than "useful" things, which go on and on. The marvelously futile, the gloriously infinitesimal, stays where it is, doesn't cease to be, living free and independent. Like the mere existence of my Odradek, which is this pin here before me, stuck in a ribbon. The mystery never becomes so clear as in the contemplation of small things that, as they move, admit that mystery's light perfectly and stop to let it pass."

By contrast, the German writer Kromberg's Odradek wasn't a miniature, but (as I said) a spectral figure: someone who posed as a poet and infiltrated the portables by traveling with them to Vienna and afterward to Prague, where he installed himself in the same hotel as Kromberg. This was the terrible Aleister Crowley, who many will know as a friend of Pessoa's, but he was other things as well—a mountaineer, a Satanist, a philosopher, lion tamer, pornographer, cyclist, heroin addict, chess player, spy, occultist—that is, a very lively Odradek, as demonstrated by the fact that he obliged the sedentary Kromberg to go abroad to Vienna and Prague. In the latter city he abducted him, used dark arts to force him into initiations of sexual magic and to scale the highest peak in Kashmir.

"What am I doing here in Kashmir?" wrote a desperate Kromberg in his travel journal, "when I like nothing better than my own hearth and to receive letters from my nomadic friends when they are off in far-flung places? I never wanted to join up with them in Vienna, but the malign influence of my Odradek drew me to that city, and then urged me onward to Prague, whence I set out for Kashmir; in Kashmir, I am currently living in the cold and in fear for my life, possessed by an inner demon that, as far as I can see, is a traveler."

Sedentary Kromberg went mad in Kashmir, losing his way, but not losing his travel journal. If we go along with certain accounts,

Kromberg, not far from the highest summit in the region, thought he'd stumbled across a hat that Pessoa had left in the snow years before. But Pessoa had never brought any hat to those icy, remote expanses, which has led more than one person to suspect that Kromberg was losing his mind, something confirmed when, on resuming his ascent, he said that he felt overcome by the flapping and cawing of crows. This in spite of the fact that there were no crows anywhere.

Finally, reaching the summit, Kromberg cried out in horror when he saw his Odradek was there, that it had overtaken him. Dressed in rigorous black, Aleister Crowley—who two years later in Seville would dissolve the secret society—greeted him with laughter, holding aloft a black flag on which, over the most ferocious skull, he had embroidered the slogan: ONWARD TO A SILKY PROSE.

Kromberg's companions tried in vain to calm him, to convince him that there was no one on the summit. That night he wrote down everything he thought he'd seen—the Portuguese hat, the crows, the Odradek with the flag—and, depositing his diary in the snow, he went out and lost himself in the darkness of the Himalayan summit, never to be seen again.

Salvador Dalí's Odradek had a markedly merry and musical air. Furthermore, it was emphatically erotic: nothing less than a self-pleasuring Chinese violin, a melodic instrument with a vibratory appendage, whose function was to be introduced—abruptly and brusquely—into the anus, but also, and preferably, into the vagina. Following insertion, an expert musician would slide his bow over the strings of the violin, playing not the first thing that came into his head, but a score expressly composed with masturbatory aims; through an astute bestowing of the frenzied sections—interspersed with moments of calm—the musician would bring the instrument's recipient to orgasm at the precise moment the rapture notes were attacked in the score.

Ramón Gómez de la Serna's Odradek wasn't exactly erotic. It showed itself in a hotel mirror in Prague, giving the writer a considerable fright: "Looking in a mirror that suddenly reflects me, I find myself truly resembling my father. Am I going to be my father? Does this mean my whole life has been a fantasy lived in another person's name? Are we nothing more than our ancestors, and never ourselves?"

He spent the day he wrote this in a state of constant unease; for a Shandy, nothing is worse than the insolent irruption of an Odradek, above all if the Odradek shows up intending to make a nuisance of itself. There were clearly also kind and timid Odradeks, but these tended to be boring. In general, Odradeks were somber, pathetic, trouble-making objects or creatures who took pleasure in frightening their hosts or victims.

That day, Gómez de la Serna had a fright like never before, but he was able to take courage and keep a sense of humor about him, and ended up giving his father's ghost the boot; he smashed every mirror in his Prague room.

But what were the portables doing in Prague if they had planned neither conference, nor manifesto, nor terrorist act, and had no plans for another party, or anything at all? I've already said that, in my opinion, the portables traveled for the mere pleasure of it, and so they could tell each other stories; but the fact is that their journey—like any novel or poem—was in constant danger of not making sense, and perhaps this was what most appealed to them about the trip.

Speaking of risks, I ought to point out that they proliferated in Prague. Very quickly, the Shandies had the unforgettable impression that at certain hours of the night or at dawn, mysterious voices not belonging to their Odradeks began to regularly whisper hushed and mysterious advice. At times, a light tremor, impossible to explain, passed through the old walls of the Jewish quarter, letting out noises that would course through the brickwork, coming out from the drainpipes. If anyone had bothered to look in that labyrinth of the Odradeks, they would have found bouquets of wilted myrtle: bridal bouquets, swept along in the unclean water, in which also hid the quiet, barely perceptible play of gestures and postures of those golems that were attached to the dangerous Odradeks.

"Dangerous, yes," Marcel Duchamp says to me on the Portbou café terrace. "So I encourage you to tread carefully with this champagne cork, apparently so well-balanced in its disingenuous equilibrium on that curtain rail: this cork *also* comes with a golem."

This memory is always evoked for me in the present tense. Suddenly I'm about to ask Duchamp what exactly he means by dangerous, but he's vanished. I look everywhere for him, including in Walter Benjamin's final resting place. Nothing but thin air. Will Duchamp turn out to be my Odradek? I thought to carry on talking about Odradeks, but now I see that the most prudent thing would be to end this chapter. Yes, perhaps it is the most advisable thing for me. After all, my history has to be a brief one, or none at all.

NEW IMPRESSIONS OF PRAGUE

> Dark the negritude
> of marble in the snow.
> —Vladimir Holan

Even I have availed myself in one chapter or another of this book of the writing procedure Blaise Cendrars used in his famed *Anthologie nègre* (*An African Saga*). Cendrars's sister Miriam showed him this procedure in her refined homage to gossip, *Inédits secrets*.

Miriam Cendrars says the *Anthologie nègre*'s creative process began in Prague during the course of a pleasant spring afternoon. Gustav Meyrink—a little unsettled since leaving Vienna because he'd yet to run into a single portable in the neighborhood—leaned out the window of his house and once more contemplated the street where he'd been born: that serpentine and lugubrious passageway at the end of which stood a Jewish cemetery, nowadays all but gone.

He stood with his elbow on the sill, thinking about what his life resembled. (Nothing, because this wasn't life. If it were, it would resemble those winters from his childhood when everything artificial won out: the brightness of lights, the closed bedrooms, the exasperation …) Suddenly, Meyrink went back to contemplating the street: the lower ground-floor shops with their lights turned on all day, overshadowed by balconied, dirty stucco facades with their volutes and heraldic emblems. Then he saw himself converted into a camera with its shutter open—passive, meticulous—and he couldn't help but think of his friends the portables, whom, for an instant, he feared he'd never see again.

This posture, so reminiscent of Berta Bocado on her balcony across from the Cabaret Voltaire, brought him luck, perhaps because it was, deep down, an intrinsically Shandy posture. Suddenly, he caught the image of a man shaving in the window across the passageway and realized right away it was Blaise Cendrars, lodged at Mrs. Pernath's guesthouse. By way of a salute, joyful Meyrink did the first few steps of an African dance, until Cendrars noticed him and, mixing some dirt in with his shaving cream, soaped his face black. Meyrink then rattled an ebony totem and Cendrars—even more euphoric than his neighbor—did some off-the-cuff drumming. For an instant, the serpentine street in Prague's Jewish quarter became the savage echo of a Congolese suburb.

It didn't take them long to connect with the mulatta Rita Malú, the Cuban actress who'd installed herself in the guesthouse on the corner and who, at that moment, was leaning out her window observing a strange passerby; this person showed a clear inclination for blackness (wearing a black hat, a black suit, a black tie, black glasses, and black shoes) and was calling out her name. In the midst of these cries, resounding in the sunken hollow of the street, the actress noticed, in the reflection of a Bohemian cut crystal, Cendrars and Meyrink exchanging dark symbols. So she whistled out a habanera, which the two Shandies immediately registered, as, of course, did the strange passerby, who, taking off his glasses and hat, revealed himself to be black Virgil.

Recognizing one another, they all brandished their respective black hats as night fell, and, in the newly inaugurated darkness, a distant echo of tam-tams could be heard from the savage tribes of future Shandies. From the solitude of their remote African cabins, they would soon see their ancient legends become portable, thanks to the *Anthologie nègre*, which Blaise Cendrars conceived the very same instant as that triumphal hat dance.

It was nothing less than an apocryphal anthology, as Cendrars's idea was to develop a book that pretended to be based on a compilation of popular African stories, when these legends were in fact a highly personal interpretation of the stories the Shandies told when they reunited in Prague.

Knowing Cendrars, the idea wasn't that surprising. Given his habit of not listening when people told him stories, he instead plucked out two or three random words, using them to construct open fictions in his mind (tales very different from the ones he actually was told).

Thus, the famed *Anthologie nègre* was born, published two years later in Paris as "a compilation of short but very vivid entries (twenty-seven), which enabled the author, for the first time in Europe, to reproduce a set of stories that missionaries and explorers had transmitted orally among us."

When it was published by the Au Sans Pareil Press in Paris, in 1927, all the French critics fell for it, greeting the work as "the first chance the lay public ever had to learn about popular African literature," when in fact what the lay public read was an African literature fabricated by Cendrars, who was able to salvage words from his portable friends' stories. The fraud went so unnoticed, the deceit was so all encompassing, that there was even a translation into Spanish by none other than Manuel Azaña.

A complete fraud. For example, the oft-repeated story "Death and the Moon"—a legend attributed to the Sande tribe and explored in great detail in the 1940's by none other than Lacan—is simply the upshot of the association of images prompted by the words moon and death (plucked by Cendrars from what Rita Malú told him the evening they met in Prague).

Rita Malú mentioned there was a full moon and, a little later, confessed she'd been feeling slightly insane in recent days. In spite of the hot weather, she'd carried on feeling terribly cold, as if Prague were being gripped by a death freeze.

Moon and death. Cendrars retained these two words when Rita Malú stopped speaking and informed her about what it was she'd just unwittingly engendered. Rita Malú fell silent, as did black Virgil and Meyrink, both of whom had been caught up in a discussion about the pros of short stories, fragments, prologues, appendices, and footnotes, and the cons of the novel. They all stopped, allowing Cendrars to narrate the legend that would become the first tale featured in the *Anthologie nègre*.

> An old man comes across a dead body in the moonlight. He assembles a great number of animals and says to them: "Who among you brave creatures will take charge of transporting this dead man and who will take charge of transporting the moon to the other side of the river?"
>
> Two turtles stepped forward: the first, who had long legs, carried the moon and made it to the opposite shore safe and sound; the other, who had short legs, took the dead man and drowned.
>
> And this is why the moon reappears day after day, and the man who dies never comes back.

This tale was punctuated by cannon fire, warning of the breaking up of the ice on the Moldova River. Spellbound, Meyrink shut his eyes to better hear Cendrars's story. But at the end of the tale, as he struggled to open his eyes again, long lines of human faces passed before him, and he saw death masks of his own ancestors: men with short, straight hair, parted hair, curly hair, long wigs, and wavy toupees. Masks approached him through the ages, and increasingly familiar lineaments gradually came together in one final face: that of the golem, which broke the ancestral chain. The darkness became an infinite, empty space, with the mother of the human race at its center.

When Meyrink finally managed to open his eyes, he communicated what he'd seen to the others. Cendrars only retained the last few words ("the mother of the human race"), using them for the title and theme of the second tale in his *Anthologie nègre*, a chronicle he attributed to the Mossi tribe:

> Three men appear before Oendé to tell him their wants. One says: I want a horse. The other says: I want dogs for

hunting in the brush. The third says: I want a woman to delight in.

Oendé gives it all to them: to the first, his horse; to the second, the dogs; to the third, a woman.

The three men leave, but rains suddenly come, preventing them from leaving the scrubland for three days. The woman cooks for the three of them. The other two men say, Let us go back to Oendé. They arrive and they ask to be given women. Oendé agrees to change the horse into a woman, and the dogs too, and the men leave. But the woman made from the horse is a glutton, the woman made from the dogs won't behave. The first woman, the one given by Oendé before, is fine: she is the mother of the human race.

This legend Cendrars kept to himself, unable to externalize it, because, as he was finishing composing it in his mind, there was a knock at the door. Salvador Dalí came in visibly excited, accompanied by Nezval and Teige, two young Czech poets who wanted to join the secret society. To judge by their radical, dazzling gazes, these two poets were very high-spirited bachelor machines. Their eyes were like highly illuminated, extraordinarily light suitcases.

Anticipating the general sentiment, black Virgil commented that he couldn't look the two Czechs in the eye because they were so dazzling. Teige hastened to say, indeed, it was true, and there was a simple explanation: their eyes were a permanent homage to Edison, the inventor of the light bulb. He then gave the floor to his colleague Nezval to announce, very emphatically, that from that moment on, for them, the sexual attractiveness of women would be based on their spectral capacity and resources, that is, on their potential dissociation, their separate carnality and luminosity. The spectral woman, he concluded, will be the woman that can be dismantled.

Teige took the floor again, showing himself to be a cutting edge Shandy by the fact that he was altogether aware of the portable Odradek-golem secret. He spoke of Prague's unusually warm air and of the presence in the city of a number of weird beings, quiet creatures pretending to sleep so no one would notice their deceptive, hostile selves. These, he said, came out when Prague's night mist covered the streets, obscuring their quiet, barely perceptible, back-and-forth gesturing and posturing: they were as profoundly dark as the spongy flesh of zombies. Additionally, he concluded, these golems were relentlessly hunted by their own "Bucharesters": beings from Romania and poor relations of Count Dracula.

Cendrars, who had listened in his own way—that is, distractedly—to the two Czech poets, then interceded to offer Nezval a pint of shandy with ice, at the same time telling him that, from his description of the woman who could be dismantled, he'd come up with a Zulu legend, "The Black Specter":

> Once upon a time, the wind was a person, specifically, a specter, until she turned into a feathered being. Because she could no longer walk, she flew. Indeed, flying, she lived on the mountainside. Once upon a time, she was a black specter, and that is why—once upon a time—she killed missionaries. Afterward, she turned into a feathered being, and from then on she flew and lived in a cave in the mountain. She goes to sleep there, wakes early and leaves; she flies far away; the next day, again, she flies far away. She comes back to her home because she feels the need for sustenance. She eats again, and again, and again; she comes back to her home, again, coming back to sleep.

As for what Teige had said, Cendrars said he didn't believe a word, but it had been useful to him in composing the fourth story of his *Anthologie nègre*, "The Zombie's Spongy Flesh" (a Babua legend). He was about to tell it, when the others asked him, in unison, to save it for later, seeing as they were all keen to go out into the streets to find as many members of the secret society as they could.

They set out on a relentless search through the bars of the Jewish quarter, but found no one. Then, they got lost on the outskirts and came to an old cemetery: a disordered jungle of jumbled tombstones piled up with dun leaves that seemed to grow out of the damp earth, vying with the wild grass to see which could grow tallest. Crows had taken over the bare trees and their cawing added to the air of nostalgic desolation about that place. On the far side of the cemetery, they saw the lights of an unsavory-looking bar: The Cabaret Zizkov. Inside the dive, someone talked to them about a foreigner who had turned into a dancing machine and was dancing alone in the bar's basement. The description of the foreigner led them all to agree that it could be Aleister Crowley, and they asked the bar's owner what they needed to do to see him.

He opened a narrow, round-arched door, and they descended a stairwell glittering with tiny crystals. The occasional lamp guided the Shandies' steps and, at the foot of the stairs, the crypt widened out. The warm and quivering air called to mind the heart of central Africa.

They went another six- or seven-hundred feet in silence. At various points the wall was punctuated by lower overtures, and there were branches off the central passageway. The crystals were constantly changing color. As they got nearer to the place where Crowley was supposedly dancing, they realized black liquid was oozing from the crystals and occasionally dripping onto their faces. At last, they arrived at the spot where the potential Shandy could be seen dancing.

It was Crowley—no doubt about it. He had chosen a splendid locale that was draped with chrome-orange crystals, one that was quite wide and with high ceilings, with tropical grasses and hummingbirds. Crowley was practicing the serpent dance, which requires the lower half of the body (from the hips to the toes) to move and nothing else. Going down into the crypt and being hit by the liquid oozing from the crystals, Crowley had turned black, and was moving his knees in at least fifteen different ways, which, even for a black person, is really quite a number.

The Shandies let out a few cries of admiration. Witnessing the chaotic conclusion to this episode—all the Shandies, smudged with black, fled the Cabaret—Cendrars took two of their cries and began constructing a new legend for his *Anthologie nègre*: a Babatúa tale in which the soul of negritude is defined as "a soul in chains, impulsive and puerile, sweet and jumpy, hungry for destruction, and, at the same time, possessed of a lucid experiential intelligence condensed in happy stories."

These happy stories are kindred in spirit to those Blaise Cendrars gathered in his *Anthologie nègre*: an impulsive, puerile book—lucid and hungry for destruction—that took him no more than five days to write. This is exactly the time it took the Shandies to disguise themselves as figures carved into the flagpoles of African huts and to regroup—secretly, ardently—in the dark, broken ice kingdoms of Prague.

POSTCARD FROM CROWLEY

But somehow every attempt always failed;
there was a traitor in the group.
—Jorge Luis Borges

"Here in Prague," Crowley wrote to Francis Picabia (who'd been awaiting word in Paris), "we came close to turning into ghosts. Seeing that more than one of us went mad and felt a desire to traverse the thick walls, I came to think we'd all end up turning into invisible beings, only able to recognize ourselves at night by our white dance scarves.

"All of it was down to Céline's antics. Having convinced himself that the conspiracy would be nothing without a traitor to jeopardize it, he decided to play that thankless role and systematically began to raise his voice during our stealthy café meetings.

"Not content with this, he began to write a book, *Le vrai nom du complot portatif*, which opened with a recollection that among the ancient Egyptians, everyone had two names: their inconsequential name (known to all) and their true or great name, which they kept hidden. After reminding the reader that the name of Rome was also secret, he went on to reveal the real name of our portable society. He did! That name which you now shudderingly recall!

"One afternoon, Valery Larbaud and five other colleagues visited Céline in his hotel and discovered this manuscript. To find it they had to go inside a tent he'd set up in the middle of his room. Enraged,

Larbaud reminded him of Quintus Valerius's fate when, in the last days of the Republic, he was executed for revealing Rome's true name.

"Duchamp, Tzara, Vallejo, everyone there, made it clear to him that he might share Quintus Valerius's fate, but Céline's response was to smile the twisted smile of one who knows how to make the foulest, most underhanded intentions smell sweet. Faced with this attitude, they burned the tent and, with it, the manuscript.

"Céline barely flinched. He seemed very comfortable in his role as the traitor, and, a few days later, he showed up again at Café Slavia, the place where we met every afternoon. He came in shouting, flanked by two professors from Madrid, even more bothersome and clingy than he was. One of them boasted of having translated Joyce into Spanish—which couldn't but fill us with misgivings since, as you well know, it was quite a while ago that Joyce parted company with us, thinking he'd have to pay a monthly membership fee. The other professor, who went by the surname Diego, claimed he was a Castilian seafarer, and proceeded to discourse on Greenland's solitary inlets, and about certain hot springs at the North Pole. An utter bore, believe me!

"We had a few truly awful days of being pursued by these clingy professors, who, in concert with the traitor, even came to defy us when we went out to Prague's purlieus, its most sequestered spots. We couldn't find a way to shake off these damned professors, who were clearly spying on us. This made many of our number feel like turning into ghosts or invisible beings. And this added to the numbers taking part in the secret expedition to the International Sanatorium, situated on the outskirts of the city, where I'm writing you from today.

"Here, away from the persecution of the traitor and his underlings, we're on a run of extraordinary, feverish creativity. All thanks to this attempt to betray us. And also in part thanks to the owner and director of the Sanatorium, whom we call Mr. Marienbad, because he doesn't want his true name revealed to anyone.

"I do not believe you'd like Marienbad. This is a man who always wears new clothes. He is a poor conversationalist, an indefatigable chatterbox. He wears an enormous, carefully sculpted beard that makes him seem all the more corpulent. He subsists on buttermilk, rice pudding, and slices of banana with butter. A lover of women, he conceals, with his unctuous ways, a brutal disposition, in turn betrayed by his flat feet, his spatula-like fingernails, his steady gaze, and ecstatic smile.

"A scientist, man of the world, and gymnastics buff, he goes around to the international gymnastics meets escorted by a number of his nurses, who, under his personal supervision, frequently win all the top prizes. Marienbad is something akin to a demagogical toiler, tirelessly churning out heavy tomes not in the least bit portable and filled with banalities; he is nonetheless growing accustomed to seeing his massive volumes published and immediately translated into several languages. Innumerable newspaper pieces have spread his name, and it would not be surprising if with his new venture, the Anonymous Kafka Society, he goes on to achieve even greater renown.

"And the thing is, Marienbad loves money. I've been able to find out that he kidnapped his wife a number of years ago, a rich Jewish hunchback with an enormous dowry, which he used to set up the International Sanatorium. Although his love of lucre is considerable, he lets us stay at the Sanatorium for free. Occasionally, one of us will make an effort and tell him a story, or simply engage him in conversation to give him a chance to let loose his balderdash. That's more than enough to keep Marienbad happy.

"He's a perfect fool, but his hospitality comes in very handy. Walter Benjamin, for instance, has used the time to start designing a promising machine that will be able to detect any book that might be boring or bothersome, that, even in miniature, wouldn't fit into a small suitcase.

"It is a very complex machine, complete with contraptions frankly unfamiliar to me: tibaida lenses, focal compartments, copper cuffs, oval cylinders, metal buttons, metal stoppers, magnetized needles, bolts, and iron jugulars.

"Walter Benjamin is sure the design will be complete in less than a month. Apparently, the method for weighing texts consists of putting a book in this cylindrical penitentiary and letting an immense, round lens look it over. Portable books will be immediately released through this black cylinder, heavy in appearance; positioned vertically on the ground, it will have a large spherical light bulb on top with the words CONTRA GRAND STYLE on it. A blue light emanating from the bulb will be visible even in bright sunlight. The book's emotional-mechanical vibration will turn the light bulb off for a fraction of a second, showing that the glass is colorless and that the light itself is actually blue. In turn, this light will reveal the inscription VIVA VERMEER at the machine's highest point—in twenty-seven different languages if possible—thus saluting effusively the recently liberated portable books.

"Otherwise, I've also managed to find out that Tristan Tzara has begun writing a brief history of portable literature: a kind of literature that, by his reckoning, is characterized by having no system to impose, only an art of living. In a sense, it's more life than literature. For Tzara, his book contains the only literary construction possible; it is a transcription made by someone unconvinced by the authenticity of History and the metaphorical historicity of the Novel. Employing greater originality than most novels, the book will offer sketches of the Shandy customs and life. Tzara's aim is to cultivate the imaginary portrait (a form of literary fantasia concealing a reflection in its capriciousness), to endeavor in the imaginary portrait's ornamentation.

"You also ought to know that Berta Bocado—moved by a sudden ambitiousness—is attempting to construct a total book: a book of books encompassing all others, an object whose virtues the years will never diminish. As ever, Bocado is being very absentminded, seeing as her book will be anything but portable.

"In fact, we're all making things. More than artists—which has a hollow, pompous ring to it—we are artisans, people who make things. An air of happy creativity pervades the rooms at the International Sanatorium. We barely see each other, since, being artisans, we take refuge in our individuality; but occasionally a polar wind blows through, bringing us all together in the central courtyard, where we smile in our thick overcoats and exchange complicit glances. A word will occasionally break the silence, and we feel ourselves straighten up like spears scaling the lofty heights and we inundate the shadows. Victory is not ours, but we fight on —silence against silence—because we know heaven never scorns ambition.

"So go the days. The occasional furtive courtyard exchange gives me an idea of how things are going with the others; this is how I found out, for example, that Scott Fitzgerald has completed a novel about a person named Gatsby, a man confronting his past as he moves inexorably into nothingness.

"George Antheil is working on his *Ballet Mécanique*, a Shandy musical par excellence. At the same time, he has turned painter and draughtsman of the miniscule: of the thousand hairs in a braid or the iridescence of a coupling, for example. He sleeps in the same room as William Carlos Williams, who, less like an American every day, entertains himself trying to solve all the arcane mysteries, with recourse to a frame made of asymmetric, revolving, concentric discs, subdivided according to the Latin words on them.

"His ex-lover, Georgia O'Keeffe, is still scheming away. She says she has been going around the theatres of an invisible city, that her imagination—voracious as gravity—is the epicenter of her convulsive passions and aversions.

"Gombrowicz is writing his first book, some nonsense to do with a ballerina: seemingly an extraordinarily brief book, that is incoherent, absurd, and, in its own way, magnificent.

"Your beloved Duchamp is drafting an essay on miniaturization as a means of fantasy. The text seems to have been conceived as a continuation of something Goethe began writing, called 'The New Melusine' (which is part of *Wilhelm Meister*), about a man who falls in love with someone—in reality a tiny woman, who has temporarily been made normal size, and who, without knowing it, is carrying a box containing the kingdom that she's the princess of. In Goethe's story the world itself is reduced to a collectible item, an object in the most literal sense. For Duchamp—like the box in Goethe's tale—a book is a fragment of the world, but it is also a small world in itself, a miniaturization of the world inhabited by the reader.

"All, as you can tell, have embarked on sharp, frenetic, desperate, portable projects—all, that is, except for Beta Bocado. Even Savinio (always the lead exponent of occasional slothfulness, that highly portable trait) has been working tirelessly and is immersed in a project as Shandean as it is unfathomable. So fed up has he become with encyclopedias that he's making his own, for his own personal use. I personally think it's a good thing; I mean, take Schopenhauer: he was so fed up with the histories of philosophy that he ended up inventing his own, for *his* own personal use.

"It seems increasingly clear to me that we, the portables, were placed on earth to express the most secret and recondite depths of our nature. This is what sets us apart from our tepid contemporaries. And I believe us to be profoundly linked to the spirit of the age, with the latent problems plaguing it and defining its tone and character. We are always dual in appearance, because of just how much we simultaneously embody the old and the new. The future that so profoundly concerns us, we are also rooted in. We have two speeds, two faces, two ways of interpreting things. We are a part of transition and flux. Versed in a new style, our language is voluble, zany, and cryptic. As cryptic as this postcard, which is nearing its end: a postcard that, at heart, claims to do no more than inform you of our great creative fever and our constant bid to exalt a love of brief literary creations; a postcard lauding free and unobstructed language and denouncing any book that makes universal or pretentious claims.

"I spoke to you about 'the most secret and recondite depths of our nature.' These corrosive secret depths are mentioned by Rimbaud in the following memorable verses: *HYDRE INTIME, sans gueules, / Qui mine et desole*. This is what afflicted him and is so disturbing to us, poorly adapted to madness as we are.

"To finish, decipher this, my dear racing car: life here in the International Sanatorium is like a murder sweet as snow, that is, cold venom covering desolate icy expanses on white nights of venerable silk.

"Yours, with more to follow, from he who idles, twirls, and dwindles upon farewell's futile brink."*

---

* For the reader intrigued about to how such a long text could fit on a postcard, I'd like to make clear that Aleister Crowley's handwriting was very, very tiny, and he succeeded in fitting all these words onto the back of a photograph of Prague, thereby fulfilling that longstanding Shandean ambition of attaining microscopic script. But the most notable thing about the postcard is that HYDRE INTIME—the portable society's secret name—appeared for the first time in writing. This greatly alarmed Picabia who immediately suspected that if there really were a traitor, it was by no means Céline, but rather Crowley himself.

ALL DAY ON THE DECK CHAIRS

Francis Picabia shouldn't have been so alarmed by Crowley's postcard. In fact the traitor's text wasn't as dangerous as it might have seemed. Properly considered, it at most betrayed something that was not overly worrying. Many of the Shandies had, at the International Sanatorium, already realized that the portable ensemble would have to disappear sooner or later; this was a fact of life and, in fact, something very much to be desired, as the conspiracy would become the stunning celebration of something appearing and disappearing with the arrogant velocity of the lightning bolt of insolence.

Duchamp, receiving a letter from Picabia at the Sanatorium informing him of the traitor's existence, tried to make him see as much. He wrote back saying that Crowley's postcard was a rousing document, a capricious text, no less, a living, breathing embodiment of Shandyism.

Indeed, the postcard displayed a sublime concern for maintaining an industrious attitude among the Shandies, and this was profoundly portable: aside from the odd period of extraordinary laziness, the portables were always keeping busy, always trying to put in more work that speculated frequently on their lives as tireless artists. A large number of the texts they produced ended up featuring curious sections with recipes for how to work: the ideal conditions, the timing, the utensils. The massive correspondence they kept up among themselves—both oral and written—was always partly animated by a desire to chronicle the work's existence: to inform, to confirm it.

Additionally, the Shandies' instincts as collectors served them well. They learned partly by collecting, as with the quotations and extracts from their daily reading, which they accumulated in notebooks they carried with them everywhere, and which they often read in their conspiratorial café meetings. Thinking was also a way of collecting for them, at least in the early days. They would meticulously note down their extravagant ideas; they'd advance mini-essays in letters to friends; rewrite plans for future projects; write down dreams; and they would carry numbered lists of all the portable books they read.

But how was it that the joyful, voluble, and zany Shandies willed themselves to become heroes? My view is that it was because of the way work can become a drug, a compulsion: "thinking is eminently narcotic," as Walter Benjamin wrote.

A need for solitude—along with bitterness about that solitude—was very common among the Shandies, joyful, voluble workers that they were. To move their work forward, they had to be solitary, or at least not form any permanent bonds. Their negative feelings toward matrimony were clearly outlined in numerous pieces of writing. Their heroes—Baudelaire, Kafka, Roussel—never married. Some of the Shandies who functioned as bachelor machines were married, but ended up thinking their marriages "fatal" to them. The world of nature, of natural relations, did not appeal to them as bachelor machines. Generally, they all hated children. Walter de la Mare actually threw his son out the window and later wrote that, for him, what is natural (when bound up by the family) ushers in the falsely subjective, the sentimental. "It was," wrote Walter de la Mare, "a bloodletting of the will, of independence, of freedom, in order to focus on the work."

The Shandy way of working meant immersion, focusing on the job. "One is either immersed, or one's thoughts float off," wrote Juan Gris. This partly explains why the Shandies installed themselves in the *Bahnhof Zoo*, a stationary submarine: they were looking for this immersion, or focus on their work. Focus, however, entails risks and ends up creating Odradeks, golems, Bucharesters. Creatures of all kinds populated the solitude of those, who, in fraught coexistence with their doppelgängers, set themselves apart in order to work.

Not even in the International Sanatorium did the Shandies manage to escape being constantly harried by these creatures—a conspiracy parallel to HYDRE INTIME—and this prompted their decision to travel to Trieste, since they thought, naively, a Mediterranean setting would disorientate their pursuers (beings that must be more disposed to mysterious Czech mists than to the diaphanous blues of the Adriatic shores). But the Shandies didn't take into account Trieste's thick, obstinate mists and, following a hazardous stay in that city, they ended up making their way back to Paris.

Upon arriving in Paris, the Shandy travelers were anxious, having confirmed the existence of the parallel plot in Trieste. They were anxious and even deformed. Meyrink, for example, looked like a cabin boy. Littbarski was dressed like a Japanese sailor. Salvador Dalí was constantly scanning the horizon for his own personal Moby Dick. Rita Malú went around dressed as a frigate. Robert Walser looked like he'd stepped straight off the *Potemkin*.

Clearly, a maritime delirium. Larbaud collected toy boats, Prince Mdivani messages in bottles, and Pola Negri photographs of whales with prey gripped between their teeth. A maritime delirium led them to mistake Paris for a gigantic country house. This led to a number of incidents with those Shandies who had remained there, but the dust didn't take long to settle. In Trieste, the portable travelers had intoned the first hymns to boredom and inconstancy in art (doubtless an anti-hysterical reaction to so much hard work). Those portables anchored in Paris's terra firma only had to make a gesture in praise of idleness for the newcomers to consider brokering a peace that would reunify the secret society.

On the day Marcel Duchamp declared that parasitism was one of the fine arts, peace was made during a dinner at La Coupole in honor of Pyecraft, an H. G. Wells character; this fictional character was portable *avant la lettre*, seeing as he lost weight but not mass, and fearing he'd float up to the sky, he left home with flat discs of lead sewn into his underclothes, lead-soled boots, and a bag full of solid lead.

Carrying my own bag full of lead, I went last week to the island of Corsica, hoping to free myself of the portables for a few days. I thought a clear consequence of my Shandy obsession and my daily dedication to writing on the subject was the creeping paralysis overtaking my Olivetti Lettera 35. I felt I'd earned a rest and the right to lose myself in an always gratifying chapter of idleness.

But it was terrible what happened to me. I saw, for example, a miniature of Napoleon—Ajaccio's local hero. I was not only immediately reminded of the Shandy enjoyment of anything small, but also the thought came to me of how small one of the portables, Robert Walser, felt when, in one of his books, he imagined himself as an infantry soldier in Bonaparte's army: "I would only be a little cog in the machine of a great design, not a man anymore ..."

Everything I saw and thought, I instantly and unavoidably related to the world of the Shandies. For instance, I lay on a deck chair by the sea and immediately remembered that the portables spent whole days on deck chairs in the city of Trieste, not to relax after working so hard, but because they had no choice if they wanted to get free of their Odradeks (these creatures wouldn't hover around as long as their hosts gave themselves over to indolence).

There was no way for me to forget about the Shandies, perhaps because my obsession was also portable; and also, after spending so many days and nights wading in Shandy waters, portability was like an ocean, seemingly endless. It carried on moving and taking me with it.

My patience ran out after I had a nightmare: slightly warped versions of Aleister Crowley's experiences in Trieste appeared to me in my dream. The nightmare had a theatrical prologue featuring infinitely immoral spectacles, which were presented to me as puritanical. When the curtain fell—with Duchamp's Shandean box-in-a-suitcase drawn on it—the character presenting the prologue disappeared, along with the immoral spectacles, and I saw silver deck chairs with golems slithering across them in pursuit of Odradeks, who, in turn, pursued femmes fatales, paddling from beach to beach in kayaks until reaching a black oily sea with professors from Madrid sailing miniature versions of ocean liners. The ships rather resembled Bucharesters rescued from the tombs of monks that had been ravaged in Sepastopol.

Suddenly, in anguish, just as the Odradeks, their golems, the femmes fatales, the Bucharesters, the monks, and the professors from Madrid all attached themselves stickily to my shoulders, I woke up. Looking in the mirror, I was relieved to see not Crowley but someone researching the secret Shandy society. No, I said to myself, I wasn't Crowley. (I repeated this one hundred times.) After that, I decided I'd go back to Barcelona that very afternoon and simply try to forget the effort involved trying to put the Shandy world behind me.

Back, then, to my brief —or, if you prefer, my interrupted—history. In *The Bucharesters*—his account of his time in Trieste—the Satanist Aleister Crowley presents his research on Bucharesters as a pretext to hammer on mercilessly about the portables, though not expressly mentioning them. Instead, he uses the enigmatic term "Bocángels."*

It's an extremely annoying book, made up of twenty-seven fragments in which Aleister Crowley unscrupulously repeats, in twenty-seven different ways, that the Bocángels spent all day on deck chairs, and with what great difficulty he bore the weight of the sticky, not at all imaginary, tribe that had attached to his shoulders. This made him sway when he walked. It's a book that seems custom made to mock anyone looking for information about the portables'

---

* "This world, republic of wind / whose monarch is an accident." These are lines from a sonnet by the Spanish poet Gabriel Bocángel (1603–1658). When I'd nearly finished my book, the daughter of Francis Picabia and Germaine Everling suggested "Bocángels" could be an indirect reference to these lines by the Spanish poet, since, according to her, the Shandies often used the term "republic of wind" for their ephemeral portable movement.

stay in the frontier city of Trieste. Here, for example, is an excerpt chosen at random:

"Trieste or the province as spectacle. I write in a bad mood after having walked the length of the Aqueduct and greeted Mr. Italo Svevo, the person least like the Bocángels of anyone. The afternoon is cold and the sky is clear, despite the *sirocco* that has been weighing on the city since this morning. It seems impossible that the consumptive carnival happening here—which began this afternoon with a *bal masque*—can resist the cold and damp. It's a poor carnival, and my playmates, my beloved Bocángels, have spurned it. The only things they like are the deck chairs. Elusive sky of Trieste! Unhappy city where I would rather not have been, because I found in an evil hour that every Odradek has its golem and every golem its Bucharester! The latter, I would like to emphasize, are beings from Romania, tiny, terrifying, and constantly attached to their masters, the golems. Here in Trieste, I would rather not be, because my own personal Odradek frequently settles on my left shoulder, accompanied by its corresponding golem, with a Bucharester also attached. On my right shoulder, my femme fatale and a professor from Madrid named Bérgamo attempt to offer the appropriate counterweight so I won't sway fiercely when I walk. Even so, I'm always swaying. The extraordinary epaulettes of my black satin jacket—black is the color of wisdom, being a concentration of all extant colors—did nothing to disguise the weight on my shoulders. On this day I decided (purely on a whim), to set out on an adventure, which, paradoxically, would be nothing if there weren't so many obstacles to overcome, or if the weight of the beings weren't so great, those beings who brazenly (resting on my shoulders) tried to impede it."

It's impossible to read Crowley and not feel constantly incredulous at all the fireworks, for instance, the unleashing of so many Bucharesters. Nonetheless, when we compare his text with Walter Benjamin's (*The Last Moment of European Intelligence*) or Man Ray's (*Travels with Rita Malú*), or Tristan Tzara's, it is surprising to see that the three concur, to a large degree, with Crowley's speculations.

"In Trieste," wrote Walter Benjamin, "the rooms of the hotel I lived in were almost all taken by Tibetan lamas who had come to the city for a pan-Buddhist convention. The number of doors left slightly ajar caught my eye. What at first seemed like coincidence ended up seeming mysterious to me. Then I found out they were members of a sect sworn never to dwell within closed spaces. I've never been able to forget the fright I felt. Someone whispered in my ear that these Tibetan lamas were, in fact, our Odradeks, and could be seen by day in the streets of Trieste, moving in the background, hidden in shacks, bordellos, cheap restaurants, pretending to be beggars, one-eyed men, out-of-work sailors, thugs, drug dealers, or doormen at brothels."

Man Ray wrote: "During our stay in Trieste, we weren't shocked by monstrousness itself, but rather just how evident it was. This is why we took refuge on the deck chairs—what a relief to regress back to infancy and discover laziness anew! We were careful not to move too much. And slowly, inexorably, it became clear that we were accompanied on our travels by the shadows of a parallel conspiracy, phantasmagorical but perceptible, led by beings that were not of flesh and blood; unlike ours, this conspiracy had an objective: it sought nothing less than the destruction of our secret society. Weird bastards they were, not of women born, dwelling, variously, in lofts, stairwells, corridors, vestibules, and also on our shoulders, even, sometimes, inside our brains."

In the opinion of Maurice Blanchot—who looks briefly at the portable phenomenon in *Faux Pas*—the "weird bastards" referred to by Man Ray were no less than the forms assumed by forgotten things; these things become distorted, unrecognizable, but nevertheless travel with us, alongside us: things in sad abandoned places, occasionally penetrating our brains, gathering together in perfect silence ("the silence of the stealthy," to quote *Tristram Shandy*, "who listen in on those, who, at one time, thought they were the only stealthy ones").

But in my opinion, there's also the chance these phantasms in the brains of the portables may have simply been the literature they produced. In any case, what's beyond question is that all the portables were aware of the existence of the parallel conspiracy, which shows they placed a very high value on art's secret demand: that the artist must know how to surprise, and be surprised by, what, though impossible, *is*.

We need only look at what Tristan Tzara says, in his *Portable History of Brief Literature*, when he confirms the existence of the parallel conspiracy: "We'd left Prague in search of a Mediterranean setting where we might shake off our relentless pursuers, but they had the temerity to arrive in Trieste ahead of us. We knew they took ether, and this delivered them faster than an express train. Their conspiracy danced at the top of a stairwell of cliff-faced steps. Meanwhile, our shoulders began to turn to rubber—as though all the water content of our bodies were dripping onto them—and seemed to want to propel us upward. Over our mouths, there was something like a mouth of ice; that is the name—Mouth of Ice—by which we began to refer to the unnamable conspiracy traveling with us and, more than once, assuming the form of that figure we find on the last and terrible page of 'Arthur Gordon Pym,' that figure whose skin was the perfect whiteness of the snow …"

The group left Trieste and went to Paris feeling sure that, with the help of the portables who'd stayed there, it might be easier to rid themselves of the Mouth of Ice; but it turned out that the perfectly snow-white conspiracy had also suffocated the Paris community of portables (using sphinxes of fire). This led many of the Shandies to take refuge at the bottom of the sea and to resume their creative endeavors in a submarine called *Bahnhof Zoo*, forgetting the deck chairs of those days of literary leisure, leaving behind the fleeting brilliance of an idle chapter.

BAHNHOF ZOO

Only two texts exist that tell us anything about the days the Shandies spent in the submarine Prince Mdivani had hired. One of them—written by the prince himself—is unreliable. The text consists of ravings, facile and absurd, seeking to describe a submarine voyage to the ends of the earth. In fact, the *Bahnhof Zoo* didn't move, nor could it, from the port of Dinard in Brittany, because it was little more than a war relic, a remnant of the first global conflict, which, before the prince took it on, had been a Chinese restaurant. The other text—the ship's log kept by Paul Klee—is far more reliable, though it does veer off at the end into a lyrical vein, casting something of a shadow over the real historical facts.

As I said, Mdivani's text is pure ravings. I don't know if he was obsessed with enthralling his readers, or if he simply wanted to make something back on his investment. Either way the prince certainly invented enjoyable—though clearly unlikely—adventures, beginning in Zanzibar and ending at the bottom of the sea in a Never-never Land. Here is a brief example of the prince's remarkable ravings: "Sailing for Balboa under a full moon one night, the clouds like mackerel bones, blurred Herculeses, mauve crepuscules, dreadful for the deranged travelers. The Panamanian coast looked like that of Wales."

As for Paul Klee, I think we should be grateful for his attempt to offer an account and excuse the way he veered off at the end, which more than anything, was due to the fact that he had recently discovered poetry. Also, he was thoughtful enough to veer off later on in the book, so we get to find out almost everything we'd want to know about the *Bahnhof Zoo*. The pages in which he veers off are actually very lovely. I enjoy taking what's expressed in them literally: the image of poor Death visiting the submarine, for example.

Klee begins his ship's log explaining where the name *Bahnhof Zoo* came from. He tells us, in Berlin in those days, the city's best known meeting point was Bahnhof Zoo. A mass of people could be seen at any time of day or night, awaiting lovers and friends beneath the clock that presided over that place. For Prince Mdivani, *Bahnhof Zoo* was the most appropriate name for his old submarine, seeing that in Berlin—beneath that clock (made in Zurich by a company called Crazy Ship)—he'd waited on a number of occasions to meet a femme fatale, who, in the end, left him feeling terribly wretched and pushed him toward the decision to hire a static submarine as consolation, where he and his portable friends could have lots of fun.

The word Zoo also evoked Noah's Ark, so similar to the submarine, since never before had such a variety of wild portable beasts gathered together. The historical partygoers from Vienna were joined at the last minute by people as distinctive as Marianne Moore, Cyril Connolly, Carla Orengo, Ezra Pound, Josephine Baker, Jacobo Sureda, Erich von Stroheim, Rozanes the jeweler, and Osip Mandelstam, among others, as well as the eccentric captain of the ship who declared his name to be Missolonghi. (He was in fact none other than Robert Walser, who, after years skirting around the edges of madness, had finally plunged into its abyss.)

"This Missolonghi," writes Paul Klee, "wore a fur-lined jacket with the collar up, a blue cap, and the look of a colossus with his curved form silhouetted against the ship's hatch, he was constantly angry with those he believed to be the longshoremen, shouting a continuous stream of invective and orders at them in an incomprehensible language."

The people he believed to be longshoremen were in fact a group of English poets, friends of Rozanes the jeweler and great admirers of Baudelaire; they gave themselves the task of overseeing the smooth running of the Macao Salon, a luxurious opium den done up like a ransacked Norwegian palace, and, along with the puppet theatre, one of the *Bahnhof Zoo*'s main attractions.

The Macao Salon—presided over by a very large witch from China—was the setting for the incident between Rita Malú and Carla Orengo. Orengo, hearing Rita Malú was in love with Francis Picabia, waited for her to enter a deep opium dream and shaved off all her hair, leaving her completely bald. Quite the scandal, a dire incident—soon to be followed by another: Max Ernst, secretly in love with Orengo and briefly touched by madness, wrote to Alfonso XIII of Spain offering him Josephine Baker's amatory services. At the same time, he proposed that he become a member of "a secret society of a portable area, a freed-up large beach of the imagination at the very center of language, needing no other key than playing along." The letter was intercepted in time by Henri Michaux, who helped Ernst regain his sanity, reminding him that it was the madness of the Shandies to make this immobile voyage at the bottom of the sea.

Michaux was convinced that submerging oneself in the depth of the port of Dinard should be understood as a journey downward. For Michaux, this meant plunging into the abyss of what sustains us, plumbing the depths of our foundations. According to him, when we go down to what is truly below, we lose our points of reference, and those audacious enough to go downward in a radical way will see for themselves how that which is above closes over them, and at the same time how that which is open in a closed space (like the *Bahnhof Zoo*) takes on a dark and distant indeterminacy.

But not all of the Shandies who submerged in search of the opium salon fully understood these perspectives that had opened up in the depths. For many of them, this was an exotic, but straightforward, trip down to a den at the bottom of the sea, until they realized it was an instinctive movement appropriate—in fact perfectly appropriate—for the portable sentiment. Furthermore—and paradoxically—the Shandy voyage could continue, immobilizing oneself in what lies beneath in order, to fully regain mobility in that which is above.

"Days of great excitement they were," writes Paul Klee, "and an awful lot of smoke. All of the portables, following previously agreed upon instructions, remembered to bring a cane with them onto the *Bahnhof Zoo*; César Vallejo's was particularly noteworthy: it was made of mahogany and at some point swelled up, and a pair of breasts appeared. It was just a cane, but, right then, it became suddenly feminine. So entranced were we by Vallejo's cane that, there beside the piano in the Macao Salon, we made it into the Shandy herald."

Cane and piano also took lead roles in one of César Vallejo's poems. Written on board the *Bahnhof Zoo*, the poem has until now been considered exceedingly hermetic when, in fact, it is a diaphanous approximation of the static voyage (downward and within) of portable opium.

"This cane is a piano that travels within, / travels by joyful leaps. / Then it meditates in iron repose, / nailed with ten horizons. // It advances. Drags itself under tunnels / beyond, under tunnels of pain, / under vertebrae naturally fugacious. // At times its tubes go, / slow yellow yearnings to live; / they go in eclipse, / and insectile nightmares delouse, / now dead to thunder, the heralds of geneses. // Dark piano, on whom do you spy / with your deafness that hears me, / with your muteness that deafens me. // Oh, mysterious pulse."

Colette, Cocteau, Varèse, and Antheil always played the piano in strict rotation, sadly, in the Macao Salon, which was always very busy. But Antheil fell in love with Pola Negri and had to be replaced by Erik Satie. In his eagerness to win the femme fatale, Antheil began carrying out oceanographic studies, sounding the watery depths in a diving suit, cataloging unknown mollusks, etc. Any activity, as long as it won her attention.

Pola Negri, initially utterly indifferent to the vivacious musician, ended up taking pity on him when he fell ill, and, then, remembering she was a femme fatale, began to seduce him in his sickbed. For a few days, they shared the same divan in the Macao Salon, until the evening when he suddenly began to notice she was afflicted by some strange ailment. Indeed, she was unwell, for she didn't know how to love. The water was killing her. The Shandies realized that they were afflicted, and so were the femmes fatales. The sun very much setting on the secret society at this point, its pangs well advanced, and the presence of this affliction, in turn, disclosed the presence of water, of nothingness, of death. George Antheil was visibly moved. "A dead woman is very weird," he said.

Death by drowning, I'd add, to paraphrase T. S. Eliot's verse homage to Pola Negri's disappearance.* Deep down (in the sea and in their consciousness), every single one of the group paid homage to this death, just as all noticed that the Odradeks were also afflicted by that strange ailment. In an opium dream, Paul Klee claimed he'd seen his Odradek take to the air from the divan shrouded in mauve smoke and flee the *Bahnhof Zoo*, swimming underwater to Saint-Malo, taking a seat on Chateaubriand's tomb and, there, at the foot of a blue anchor painted onto a whitewashed wall, watching the ships go by, he took a revolver from its pocket, placed it in his mouth, and pulled the trigger. "For a moment," writes Paul Klee, "the Odradek remained seated, looking at the grave, the radiance of the sea and the ships. But soon after, everything, including him, vanished into the Breton sunset."

This story and a great many more, came to be staged in the puppet theater of the submarine's Malabar Salon. All of the Shandies remembered the celebrated beginning of Goethe's *Wilhelm Meister*, in which the eponymous character tells of being introduced to the marvelous world of hand-spectacle. (As a child, his father gave him a portable puppet theater. So there was no way the *Bahnhof Zoo* could do without the fascinating puppet universe. To the portables, the puppets were useful as a metaphor for being happy and in motion; the puppets' actions didn't depend on their own consciousness. They were able to postulate the starting points of a wise pilgrimage among the crags and cliffs of knowledge, the high illuminations of grace. The puppets served, additionally, as a way for Shandies to tell

* "The Shady Shandy," a Spanish version of which appeared in the *Ocnos* anthology (Barcelona, 1967), translated by Jaime Gil de Biedma.

71

their continuous stories, an essential pleasure in all voyages.

Some of these stories were especially interesting, such as the one presented by René Daumal, who reflected on the death of literature using an old wardrobe. His spectacle concluded with the following wise words, uttered by a puppet meant to be the Phantom of the Opera: "Properly considered, literature comes alive when someone, sitting down to write a simple letter, hesitates for a few moments, wondering how to make what he proposes to say credible. And in the worst-case scenario—taking into account that people will one day cease to write letters—literature will still never die, that is, as long as the poets know how to read as well as how to write: Poets will never die, precisely because they die."

Death, the language of death, language, and the death of language were the most common themes of the performances at the Malabar. And when word came of Jacques Rigaut's disappearance in Palermo, a dramatization of his death by Georgia O'Keeffe became a favorite among the portable audience.

It was narrated in a cruel and coldhearted manner, seeing that Jacques Rigaut was presented on stage going mad and finally throwing himself grotesquely onto a mattress made to resemble a canoe, paddling upstream against death. Tasteless and unfair, it provoked critical responses. Frederico García Lorca's stood out in particular; without ever having personally met Rigaut, he decided to rise to his defense and put on one of the *Bahnhof Zoo*'s loveliest ever puppet shows.

García Lorca moved the action from Palermo to Granada, specifically to the Alhambra Hotel, where Rigaut—wan and Andalucian—playfully experienced his own death accompanied by the tragic tap dance of several ballerina "pill puppets" (their sparkling blue blinded everyone in the audience). Following the dazzling, barbiturate dance of death, an electrical contraption appeared on stage, invented by Lorca himself, its objective when turned on being to radiate a very intense cold that would chill the blood. At that moment—and while the audience's only thought was to find some way to wrap up warm—the curtain fell, with a painting on it by Lorca of an infinite yellow-sand avenue. In the foreground, where the avenue began, a Sudanese marionette could be seen: a black beggar woman with gray matted hair singing "Nessun Dorma." While practicing the art of divination, she announced the Shandy conspiracy's dark future.

Another of the most interesting puppet shows came courtesy of Stephan Zenith, who turned the puppets into quick-change artists, using them to represent (with remarkable brevity and ingenuity) the most extraordinary parts of the most select Shandy biographies. For every part, a different costume. All at high speed, worthy of Fregoli. There were six or seven scenes for each biography, seeing that life—sorry to say—isn't worth much more than that.

After these speedy transformations came the final scene, which was the same for everyone: A skeleton with a scythe appeared, pretending not to seek its victim but knowing it would actually find him, the two then bumped into each other, and Death would mow down the portable's abbreviated life at the roots.

This scene always brought a sad and resigned applause from the audience. The fact is, if one thing had become evident, there aboard the *Bahnhof Zoo*, it was that the conspiracy could, at any moment, enter into its final agony: there were signs now that Death was tightening its net.

Poor, powerless Death. "It boarded the submarine," says Klee, "only to scramble away in dismay. And sailed for dry land, navigating terrifying Breton rocks along the way." We come to the end of Klee's ship's log: not wanting to go into detail about why the immobile voyage reached its end, he resorts to poetic imagery telling us that, in spite of Death's visit, the portables managed to frighten Death away, thereby delaying the final agonies of their heroic conspiracy.

I've always enjoyed taking literally what Paul Klee tells us at the end of his ship's log. It's always been pleasing to me to believe that, indeed, Death showed up in the early hours, with its skeleton and its scythe, curious to find out what was going on inside that submarine. Three surprises awaited It. The first was finding that what was aboard the *Bahnhof Zoo* was reminiscent of Livy's splendid description of the destruction of Alba Longa with its inhabitants roaming the streets, bidding farewell to the stones. The second surprise was seeing rainfall at the bottom of the sea and "a thick tear falling, deliberately overflowing itself, like a ghost of itself, making as though to extinguish itself with a vague gesture of forgetting, in a reasonable sea, where the rain was slow and slanting, and what was weeping was prose ..."

As for the third surprise, it was considerable, and put to flight poor, powerless Death. Death decided to go into the Malabar Salon, and there discovered its puppet status. Death sat down and, before fleeing in terror, smoked some opium, sweating buckets, and, like any other spectator, impatiently awaited the end of the final scene to find out if there was any ever after.

THE ART OF INSOLENCE

I don't know why they disembarked from the *Bahnhof Zoo*. Most likely it was fatigue that forced them up to the surface again. Fatigue and also a certain anguish, which is what we can gather from a document found in a false-bottom trunk stored in a loft in the house Crowley would later own; the document was discovered by the house's subsequent owner, the Singer sewing-machine magnate, Edward Clark (also an ardent student of the history of the portable conspiracy), who died in strange circumstances a few days after finding the document and writing a brief text, *A Shandy Draws the Map of His Life*. This text, it seems, was inspired by some images from his dream about the years that Walter Benjamin toyed with the idea of making a map of his life.

Benjamin imagined this map to be gray and portable; he even designed a system of colored signs clearly marking the homes of his Shandy friends, the cafés and bookshops where they met, the single-night hotels, the underwater light of European libraries, the paths leading to different schools, and the graves they saw filling up.

"To lose one's way in a city," wrote Walter Benjamin, "as one loses one's way in a forest, requires some schooling.... This art I acquired rather late in life; it fulfilled a dream, of which the first traces were labyrinths on the blotting papers in my school notebooks. No, not the first traces, for there was one earlier that outlasted the others: the way into this labyrinth."

The Shandy conspirators' way into the labyrinth, it seems to me, is the central theme in Edward Clark's document, the ideal complement to that document Clark found in the false-bottom trunk in the loft of the house that once belonged to Crowley. This document was a lecture on the anguish of the portable writer, and had originally been written by Bruno Schulz, who intended to read it out loud on the *Bahnhof Zoo*. But all evidence points to the fact that it fell into the hands of Crowley, who subtly altered it and, passing himself off as the poetess Elsa Tirana (a pseudonym for Cléo de Mérode, mistress to King Leopold of Belgium), read it in consummate cross-dress at Seville's Ateneo, during the Góngora tribute that was set up by the Spanish Generation of '27 poets.

The lecture considered anguish—as I said, the original text was by Schulz—but Crowley injected some sentences disclosing to the world the existence of the secret Shandy society. A comprehensive betrayal. To that end, Crowley backed up his reading by showing a crude imitation of Benjamin's dream map. Among those in attendance, mingled with a sizeable delegation of professors from Madrid, a large number of Shandies could be seen listening cheerfully to the revelation of their secret, even though this meant the certain dismantling of all that was portable. Each had on their persons a thermometer and was accompanied by a black man or woman from Port Actif.

It should surprise no one that the Shandies were extremely cheerful. As previously eluded to, they had understood early on that if they wanted the conspiracy to work better, it first had to vanish from the map: that is, the conspiracy needed to appear in the eyes of the world like the stunning celebration of something appearing and disappearing with the arrogant velocity of the lightning bolt of insolence. And we must be mindful that insolence, when it becomes manifest, does so always in relation to others, as part of a movement that is mindful—intensely mindful—of the other. It is the expression of a rebellious, scandalous, immortal ego imposing itself as a way of exposing itself.

Grasping all of this led the conspirators to a pact of solidarity entailing a series of essential obligations, such as, for example, not visibly extending the existence of the conspiracy and, in brief, showing themselves swift and masterly in the art of abbreviation. This led them to close ranks against Crowley the traitor, which, in turn, gave him license to expose them to the world.

What follows are certain interesting paragraphs the false Tirana read in Seville: "I'm here to say I don't like you at all, mainly because there are twenty-seven of you, which is unacceptable, given that this number belongs exclusively to us.... As you can see, Shandy writers have a touch of the exorbitant, of the unacceptable about them. It's both laughable and pathetic that to become manifest, anguish requires the work of a portable, sitting at a desk, writing letters on a piece of paper. Shocking it may seem, but only in the way that a prerequisite for a madman in his solitude is the presence of a sane witness.... Anguish means I no longer have anything to say about anything, but it would haunt me no less if I tried to give this lecture a justifying aim.... This aim could consist of me standing in front of you and saying a few words to try to forget, momentarily, my anguish. Clearly, I haven't managed that. This lecture could have me acting like a traitor and unmasking the presence of the many Shandies among the respectable public. Clearly, I *have* managed that.... And I am pleased, to tell the truth, because all that is portable will never rear its head again. Having come this far, I'm off, and I'll take my Portuguese hat and my intimate hydra with me. I believe I've written these words as the day draws its images, whispering over them, never to return."

When the lecture finished, it was roundly applauded by the professors from Madrid, seeing that—as Elsa Tirana was one of Marinetti's foremost disciples—they thought the lecture must be avant-garde. But their applause only infuriated the portables, who decided to go around spreading all manner of malicious lies about the professors: a breakneck procession of gossip that sowed panic in the Ateneo.

Emilio Prados, in an attempt to quell that orgy of calumny and gossip, went over to the person he thought was the leader of that insolent group, García Lorca, and took issue with the lowliness of gossip in literary terms. Glaring at Prados and leaning on the shoulder of the beautiful black woman he had with him, Lorca explained that Marcel Proust wrote novels comprised solely of gossip and the same went for Henry James.

Along came Duchamp, a refreshing glass of shandy in hand, explaining to Prados that they only told stories so someone would repeat them, and that they would stop telling them when they were no longer fresh. If the stories ceased to be fresh, that was because, upon being heard, they no longer spun and wove. Then Luis Cernuda, grinning ear to ear, joined his Shandy colleagues, adding: "Let me tell you: gossip is part and parcel of this transitory state; a link in a chain whose other links are only partial reiterations. Gossip— narrative as pure transitoriness—also presents the impossibility of identical repetition, the inevitability of endless transformation."

Prados was stunned by these words and cast around for help; several professors came over and surrounded García Lorca. Someone took advantage of this moment to take a photograph, in which the Granadian poet can be seen, looking like a detainee, between Alberti and Chavás.

But then all the black men and women broke into song. It was quite the scandal, the triumph of insolence as fine art. For a few minutes the gossip reached a crescendo, between songs and fireworks that were set off all around the room. Only then did Dámaso Alonso sense that Shandyism could literally be true. He went over to Rita Malú to ask if she was also part of the portable conspiracy.

"Impossible," said Rita Malú, "because the Shandies are all angels, and I am not." He then inquired as to where those angels lived. In *Letters from Mogadishu*, Rita Malú says that she gave the following answer, putting him on the right track: "Men, you men, your testicles are brimming with angels."

A phrase that puts us precisely on the right spermy track as to the potential energy, the very essence of Shandyism, which didn't disappear even when Crowley—after leaving the Ateneo—opened the window of his Seville residence and, with a histrionic flourish, dissolved the secret society. It was an energy that didn't disappear but rather, in its scattering, became more potent; the experience of literature is living proof of this scattering, proof of that which escapes unity for good reason. We shouldn't be surprised, therefore, that the scattering of the secret society—and with it, of portable literature—would mark the moment when it began to approximate itself and finally began to be genuinely portable.

A SHANDY DRAWS THE MAP OF HIS LIFE

> "I travel to know the geography of myself."
> —Journal entry of a madman,
> quoted by Marcel Réja in
> *L'art chez les fous* (Paris, 1907)

Together, all the Shandies make up the face of one imaginary Shandy. The incidents that configured their tragic face can be read in the lines of this portable portrait, the map of their imaginary life. In this face—in all the Shandy faces for that matter—there have been deep lines since youth, lines that will gradually widen until they become emptiness itself. This unique mask—the synthesis of all portable masks—will be found in the tenuous light of a visit to Seville that pays homage to the majesty of time. (Time has ravaged this singular, solitary face, the face of the last Shandy.)

In most of the portraits his eyes are downcast. His right hand is held near to the face. The oldest example I know shows him in 1924, not long after his nervous breakdown beside the enormous towering rock where the concept of eternal recurrence came to Nietzsche. He has dark, wavy hair and a high forehead. He looks young, almost handsome; his eyes downcast—with the gentle, dreamy gaze of the shortsighted—seemingly floating toward the picture's lower left-hand corner.

In the photograph of him at the party in Vienna, his wavy hair has receded just a little, but no trace of his youth and beauty remain;

the face has flattened out, and the upper torso seems not just puffed, but burly, enormous. The hand—clenched into a fist with the thumb between two figures—covers his mouth, the fleshy lower lip. The gaze is opaque, or simply more inward, and there are books behind his head.

In another photograph, taken at the bottom of the sea, he's standing immersed in thought in the *Bahnhof Zoo*, looking very elderly in a white shirt, tie and trousers over which dangles the chain of his pocket watch; his disheveled figure gives the camera a truculent look.

Finally, in the clear light of a room in Seville, he is consulting the final pages of a volume held open on a table by his left hand; it's as though he's looking toward the lower left-hand corner of the photograph; he seems, surprisingly, much younger than three years before and gives the impression of having achieved his goal of becoming a proficient reader of maps, composed of imaginary streets along which one can happily drift; it's as though his gaze were already wandering through the final pages of that volume where he might have found the map of his life, a labyrinth in which every connection with a Shandy conspirator may be figured as an entrance into the morass of the portables' invisible city, a space where losing oneself takes practice. The art of wandering the streets of the imagination reveals the true nature of the history of the modern city and leads us to the doors of the singular building where the last Shandy lives.

This person is someone who approaches life like a space in which to draw a map, someone who in Port Actif—when the secret society was being founded—was already considered melancholic, cut out for no other human state than solitude. (That is, solitude in the great metropolis or spent as a wanderer, fully at leisure to daydream.) This person considers himself melancholic, since he came to earth when Saturn—the slowest turning planet, the planet of digression and dilation—was in the ascendant. And under the auspices of this sign, he gets lost—like any good wanderer—in the labyrinth of Odradeks, with the Moldova ice slowly breaking up.

Since being slow is a feature of a melancholy temperament, the

Shandy spends all day in Trieste on deck chairs. His slowness comes out in the way he reads the world. The melancholic person knows how best to read the world precisely because he is obsessed by death. Albeit, on the submarine, his vision of death gives him the sense that it is his melancholy that the world gives in to.

Once he gets to Seville, he considers the way that the more lifeless things are, the more potent and ingenious the mind contemplating them becomes; inert in the face of approaching disaster, in his melancholy, he is galvanized by the passion that exceptional objects awaken. He begins collecting books as well as passions, he knows that the hunt for books, like sexual pursuit, enriches the geography of pleasure. This is another reason to drift in the world. As well as first editions and distinctively baroque books, he collects miniatures: postcards, pennants, toy soldiers.... The love of small things underlies his liking for brevity in literature; his library is full of short books evocative of the cities he has become familiar with: Port Actif, Paris, Palermo, New York, Vienna, Ajaccio, Prague, Trieste, Seville.

Prague, on the map. This is the city in which the Shandy learns to journey around inside his room while sitting at his desk, staring at a blank page, and receiving a visit from his Odradek. Hunched over his papers and wrestling with the work at hand, the Shandy notices that a darker and inferior being has settled on his shoulder, an Odradek that attacks his soul, squeezing, narrowing yet rejuvenating it, and, after a fashion, taking years off of it. At first, the Shandy evades this violation by pretending no one's visited him, but soon he comes to understand that this spreading of a semi-dark inferiority over his person is the most pointed and most creative of all violations; so he gives in to his Odradek, knowing he'll become lost with him in the chaos that will finally give birth to portable literature.

Palermo, on the map. This is the city in which the Shandy life is a drawing of death. The Shandy will never go to Palermo, he'll send someone in his place: a suicidal emissary who will convert a Sicilian hotel into a forbidden place in his memory.

Paris, on the other hand, is the underwater light of the days of his portable training. Silver bridges over the Seine link the intricate paths of a journey leading him through the days of his Parisian apprenticeship, to a convoy of stars, and from there, back down to earth once more, to the opaque nothing of an insolent farewell in Seville.

Seville is not on the map. On this southern tip, the last Shandy—a Saturnine hero with his ruins, his miniatures, his defiant visions and his relentless penumbra—thinks his intensity, his exhaustive melancholic attention will set natural limits on how long he can continue to elucidate his ideas on literature and life; he decides to conclude the book he's working on in order to finish just in time: before it self-destructs. This is the decision of a person who knows that history in its true countenance swiftly passes by, and that the past can only be retained as an image emitting—like the lightning bolt of insolence, in its visible moment—a radiance that will never be seen again.

Only because the past is dead are we able to read it. The last Shandy knows that only because it is fetishized in physical objects can history be understood. Only because it is a world can a book be entered. For the last Shandy—for whom his book is another space in which to wander—his real impulse when people look at him is to lower his gaze, bow his head toward his notebook, look off into a corner, or better yet, hide his head behind the portable wall of his book.

ESSENTIAL BIBLIOGRAPHY

Beach, Sylvia. *Shakespeare and Company*. New York: Harcourt Brace, 1959.

Blanchot, Maurice. *Faux pas*. Paris: Éditions Gallimard, 1943. (English-language edition: *Faux Pas*, tr. Charlotte Mandell. Stanford: Stanford University Press, 2001.)

Canell, Skip. *Pessimism*. New York: Indolence Editions, 1958.

Céline, Louis-Ferdinand. *La vrai nom du complot portatif (The True Name of the Portable Conspiracy)*, c. 1924. Manuscript disappeared in Prague.

Cendrars, Blaise. *L'Anthologie nègre*. Paris: Correa, 1947. (English-language edition: *The African Saga*, tr. Margery Williams Bianco. New York: Payson & Clarke, 1927.)

Cendrars, Miriam. *Inédits secrets (Unpublished Secrets)*. Paris: Éditions Gallimard, 1969.

Crowley, Aleister. *Os Bucharestis (The Bucharesters)*. Oporto: Porto Editorial, 1948. Original presumed lost.

Huidobro, Vicente. *El sabotaje de lo instituido (Sabotaging the Establishment)*. Buenos Aires: Editorial Sudamericana, 1962.

Klee, Paul. *Tagebücher* (diaries). Cologne: Verlag M. DuMont, 1957.

Kromberg, Hermann. *Tagebücher*, ed. Aleister Crowley. Vienna: Keuschnig, 1929.

Littbarski, Werner and Valery Larbaud. *Die Shüsse eines Junggesellen*. Vienna: Keuschnig, 1930. (English-language edition: *A Bachelor Opens Fire*. Glasgow: Surrealist Armouries Press, 1960.)

Malú, Rita. *Cartas desde Mogadishu* (*Letters from Mogadishu*). Havana: Editorial Espuela de la Plata, 1969.

Man Ray. *Travels with Rita Malú*. New York: Reynal & Hitchcock, 1947.

de la Mare, Walter. *Biographical Memoirs of Extraordinary Shandies*. Middlesex: Penguin, 1951.

O'Keeffe, Georgia. *Pictures* (memoir). Princeton: Princeton University Press, 1951.

Picabia, Francis. *Veuves et militaires* (*Widows and Soldiers*). Forthcoming from Corti Bookshop Press (11 rue de Medicis, Paris).

Rigaut, Jacques. *Agence générale du suicide* (*General Suicide Agency*). Paris: Le Terrain Vague, 1974. (Included in *Four Dada Suicides*, tr. Terry Hale, Iain White, et al. London: Atlas Press, 1995.)

Sterne, Laurence. *The Life and Opinions of Tristram Shandy, Gentleman*. New York: Modern Library Classics, 2004.

Typ(h)on, Ant(h)ony. *In Praise of Discomposure*. (With prologue by Jorge Luis Borges and Maria Kodama and epilogue by Virginia Klimt.) New Orleans: Klimt Editions, 1983.

Tzara, Tristan. "Histoire portative de la littérature abregé" ("A Portable History of Brief Literature"), in *Sept manifestes Dadá. L'espion des realistes et une histoire inédite*. Paris: J. J. Pauvert, 1963. (English-language edition: *Seven Dada Manifestos and Lampisteries*, tr. Barbara Wright. London: John Calder, 1977.)

New Directions Paperbooks — a partial listing

Martín Adán, The Cardboard House
César Aira
  An Episode in the Life of a Landscape Painter
  Conversations
  Ghosts
Will Alexander, The Sri Lankan Loxodrome
Paul Auster, The Red Notebook
Gennady Aygi, Child-and-Rose
Honoré de Balzac, Colonel Chabert
Djuna Barnes, Nightwood
Charles Baudelaire, The Flowers of Evil*
Bei Dao, The Rose of Time: New & Selected Poems*
Nina Berberova, The Ladies From St. Petersburg
Rafael Bernal, The Mongolian Conspiracy
Max Blecher, Adventures in Immediate Irreality
Roberto Bolaño, By Night in Chile
  Distant Star
  Last Evenings on Earth
  Nazi Literature in the Americas
Jorge Luis Borges, Labyrinths
  Seven Nights
Coral Bracho, Firefly Under the Tongue*
Kamau Brathwaite, Ancestors
Sir Thomas Browne, Urn Burial
Basil Bunting, Complete Poems
Anne Carson, Glass, Irony & God
Horacio Castellanos Moya, Senselessness
Louis-Ferdinand Céline
  Death on the Installment Plan
  Journey to the End of the Night
Inger Christensen, alphabet
Jean Cocteau, The Holy Terrors
Peter Cole, The Invention of Influence
Julio Cortázar, Cronopios & Famas
Albert Cossery, The Colors of Infamy
Robert Creeley, If I Were Writing This
Guy Davenport, 7 Greeks
Osamu Dazai, No Longer Human
H.D., Tribute to Freud
  Trilogy
Helen DeWitt, Lightning Rods
Robert Duncan, Selected Poems
Eça de Queirós, The Maias
William Empson, 7 Types of Ambiguity
Shusaku Endo, Deep River
Jenny Erpenbeck, Visitation
Lawrence Ferlinghetti
  A Coney Island of the Mind

Thalia Field, Bird Lovers, Backyard
F. Scott Fitzgerald, The Crack-Up
  On Booze
Forrest Gander, As a Friend
  Core Samples From the World
Henry Green, Pack My Bag
Allen Grossman, Descartes' Loneliness
John Hawkes, The Lime Twig
Felisberto Hernández, Lands of Memory
Hermann Hesse, Siddhartha
Takashi Hiraide, The Guest Cat
Yoel Hoffman, The Christ of Fish
Susan Howe, My Emily Dickinson
  That This
Bohumil Hrabal, I Served the King of England
Sonallah Ibrahim, Stealth
  That Smell
Christopher Isherwood, The Berlin Stories
Fleur Jaeggy, Sweet Days of Discipline
Gustav Janouch, Conversations With Kafka
Alfred Jarry, Ubu Roi
B.S. Johnson, House Mother Normal
James Joyce, Stephen Hero
Franz Kafka, Amerika: The Man Who Disappeared
Alexander Kluge, Cinema Stories
Laszlo Krasznahorkai, Satantango
  The Melancholy of Resistance
Mme. de Lafayette, The Princess of Clèves
Giuseppe Tomasi di Lampedusa
  Places of My Infancy
Lautréamont, Maldoror
Denise Levertov, Selected Poems
Li Po, Selected Poems
Clarice Lispector, The Hour of the Star
  Near to the Wild Heart
  The Passion According to G. H.
Luljeta Lleshanaku, Child of Nature
Federico García Lorca, Selected Poems*
  Three Tragedies
Nathaniel Mackey, Splay Anthem
Stéphane Mallarmé, Selected Poetry and Prose*
Norman Manea, Captives
Javier Marías, Your Face Tomorrow (3 volumes)
  While the Women Are Sleeping
Thomas Merton, New Seeds of Contemplation
  The Way of Chuang Tzu
Henri Michaux, Selected Writings
Dunya Mikhail, Diary of a Wave Outside the Sea

Henry Miller, The Air-Conditioned Nightmare
Big Sur & The Oranges of Hieronymus Bosch
The Colossus of Maroussi
Yukio Mishima, Confessions of a Mask
Death in Midsummer
Eugenio Montale, Selected Poems*
Vladimir Nabokov, Laughter in the Dark
Nikolai Gogol
The Real Life of Sebastian Knight
Pablo Neruda, The Captain's Verses*
Love Poems*
Residence on Earth*
Charles Olson, Selected Writings
George Oppen, New Collected Poems (with CD)
Wilfred Owen, Collected Poems
Michael Palmer, Thread
Nicanor Parra, Antipoems*
Boris Pasternak, Safe Conduct
Kenneth Patchen
Memoirs of a Shy Pornographer
Octavio Paz, Selected Poems
A Tale of Two Gardens
Victor Pelevin, Omon Ra
Saint-John Perse, Selected Poems
Ezra Pound, The Cantos
New Selected Poems and Translations
Personae
Raymond Queneau, Exercises in Style
Qian Zhongshu, Fortress Besieged
Raja Rao, Kanthapura
Herbert Read, The Green Child
Kenneth Rexroth, Songs of Love, Moon & Wind
Written on the Sky: Poems from the Japanese
Keith Ridgway, Hawthorn & Child
Never Love a Gambler
Rainer Maria Rilke
Poems from the Book of Hours
Arthur Rimbaud, Illuminations*
A Season in Hell and The Drunken Boat*
Guillermo Rosales, The Halfway House
Evelio Rosero, The Armies
Joseph Roth, The Emperor's Tomb
Jerome Rothenberg, Triptych
Ihara Saikaku, The Life of an Amorous Woman
William Saroyan
The Daring Young Man on the Flying Trapeze
Albertine Sarrazin, Astragal
Jean-Paul Sartre, Nausea
The Wall

Delmore Schwartz
In Dreams Begin Responsibilities
W.G. Sebald, The Emigrants
The Rings of Saturn
Vertigo
Aharon Shabtai, J'accuse
Hasan Shah, The Dancing Girl
C.H. Sisson, Selected Poems
Gary Snyder, Turtle Island
Muriel Spark, The Ballad of Peckham Rye
A Far Cry From Kensington
Memento Mori
George Steiner, My Unwritten Books
Antonio Tabucchi, Indian Nocturne
Pereira Declares
Yoko Tawada, The Bridegroom Was a Dog
The Naked Eye
Dylan Thomas, A Child's Christmas in Wales
Collected Poems
Under Milk Wood
Uwe Timm, The Invention of Curried Sausage
Charles Tomlinson, Selected Poems
Tomas Tranströmer
The Great Enigma: New Collected Poems
Leonid Tsypkin, The Bridge over the Neroch
Summer in Baden-Baden
Tu Fu, Selected Poems
Frederic Tuten, The Adventures of Mao
Regina Ullmann, The Country Road
Jane Unrue, Love Hotel
Paul Valéry, Selected Writings
Enrique Vila-Matas, Bartleby & Co.
Dublinesque
Elio Vittorini, Conversations in Sicily
Rosmarie Waldrop, Driven to Abstraction
Robert Walser, The Assistant
Microscripts
The Tanners
Eliot Weinberger, An Elemental Thing
Oranges and Peanuts for Sale
Nathanael West
Miss Lonelyhearts & The Day of the Locust
Tennessee Williams, Cat on a Hot Tin Roof
The Glass Menagerie
A Streetcar Named Desire
William Carlos Williams, In the American Grain
Selected Poems
Spring and All
Louis Zukofsky, "A"
Anew

*BILINGUAL EDITION

For a complete listing, request a free catalog from New Directions, 80 8th Avenue, New York 10011
or visit us online at ndbooks.com